IMMENSEE

LENZ

A VILLAGE ROMEO AND JULIET

G000065637

IMMENSEE
Theodor Storm
Translated by Ronald Taylor

LENZ
Georg Büchner
Translated by Michael Hamburger

A VILLAGE ROMEO AND JULIET
Gottfried Keller
Translated by Ronald Taylor

JOHN CALDER · LONDON
RIVERRUN PRESS · NEW YORK

This edition published in Great Britain in 1985 by
John Calder (Publishers) Ltd
18 Brewer Street, London W1R 4AS

and in the USA in 1985 by
Riverrun Press Inc
1170 Broadway, New York, NY 10001

This edition first published in 1966 by
Calder & Boyars Ltd, London

Copyright © Translation of *Immensee* John Calder (Publishers) Ltd
   1966, 1985
Copyright © Translation of *Lenz* Michael Hamburger 1947, 1985
Copyright © Translation of *A Village Romeo and Juliet* John Calder
   (Publishers) Ltd 1966, 1985

ALL RIGHTS RESERVED

ISBN 0 7145 0561 7

No part of this publication may be reproduced, stored in a retrieval
system, or transmitted in any form, by any means, electronic, mechanical,
photocopying or otherwise, except brief extracts for the purpose of
review, without the prior permission of the copyright owner and
publisher.

Any paperback edition of this book, whether published simultaneously
with, or subsequent to, the hardback edition is sold subject to the
condition that it shall not, by way of trade, be lent, resold, hired out or
otherwise disposed of, in any form of binding or cover other than that in
which it is published.

Printed and bound in Italy by
Stabilimento Poligrafico Cappelli

CONTENTS

	Page
IMMENSEE by Theodor Storm	
INTRODUCTION	9
PRINCIPAL DATES IN THE LIFE OF THEODOR STORM	12
IMMENSEE	13
LENZ by Georg Büchner	
INTRODUCTION	55
PRINCIPAL DATES IN THE LIFE OF GEORG BÜCHNER	58
LENZ	59
A VILLAGE ROMEO AND JULIET by Gottfried Keller	
INTRODUCTION	97
PRINCIPAL DATES IN THE LIFE OF GOTTFRIED KELLER	100
A VILLAGE ROMEO AND JULIET	101

IMMENSEE

THEODOR STORM

Translated by Ronald Taylor

INTRODUCTION

THE stories and the lyrical poetry of Theodor Storm are as unproblematical as their author's life was uneventful. He was born in 1817 in the little, grey fishing town of Husum, in the province of Schleswig, and ended his working days as governor of that same place. Only twice did he leave his native province for any extended time: as a student, when he had been to Lübeck, Kiel and Berlin; and as a patriot, when he was virtually forced into exile under the Danish occupation of Schleswig and did not return for eleven years. And at all times his life was governed by the values that one would expect to result in, or to be expressive of, such a mode of existence: on the personal plane, a devotion alike to the responsibilities and the joys of family life, and beyond this, an intense pride in the sturdy North German independence of his province, particularly in the face of Danish aggressiveness.

Both in its nature and in its scope his literary work is the proper complement to his life—sincere, honest, uncomplicated, direct. As a lyric poet he modelled his style on Eichendorff, from whom he received the vision of a world admittedly not perfect in its manifest forms —witness his poems of political protest—but assuredly God-given and thus true.

As a narrative writer he stands equally in the Romantic tradition in those stories—among them *Immensee*— that descend from the period of his most unmistakably personal lyric poetry, that is, between 1840 and 1865; but in later life the surface of his stories became harder and his tone of voice more severe.

At their most characteristic, both Storm's lyric and narrative writings are sustained by a mood of reminiscence, of meditation, of 'emotion recollected in tranquillity'. Their subjects are private and intimate, their justification and their validity personal; he himself characterised the novelettes composed in this spirit as 'stories of situation'. Their strength lies in their honesty; their besetting danger is sentimentality, a sentimentality inseparable from their genesis in a desire to escape in the imagination from what Storm once called 'this agonising reality'. He softens the jagged outlines of this reality by drawing across them a veil of dreams and illusions, so that what he now observes, from an imagined distance in time or place, partakes of the quality of an ideal and loses much of the particularity of a 'real', here-and-now situation.

Immensee, written in 1849, belongs in this context. Its characters live in the middle-class world of Storm's experience, contain their activities within its approved, conventional limits, yet seem almost too frail, too *weltfremd* to represent life in that world or to deal with its real problems. The old man, sadly reminiscing on an unfulfilled past; the sensitive, romantic youth who collects flowers and writes poetry; the simple, virtuous, rather colourless girl of childhood memory, and her pragmatic, utterly unromantic mother—these are typical creatures of Storm's poetic world. The tone is subdued, the manner unhurried, the outcome of the events unchallenged. The emotional range is narrow—

but perhaps it is the concentration forced by this very narrowness that gives Storm his particular place of affection as a minor master in the German literature of the nineteenth century.

R. T.

PRINCIPAL DATES IN THE LIFE OF THEODOR STORM

1817 Born on September 14th in Husum, Schleswig.

1835–36 Completed his school education at the Katharineum in Lübeck.

1837–42 Studied law at the universities of Berlin and Kiel.

1843 Return to Husum as a local government servant.

1846 Marriage to Constanze Esmarch.

1848–50 Schleswig-Holstein War of Liberation against Denmark.

1851 First published work: *Sommergeschichten und Lieder*, a collection of poems and short stories, including *Immensee*.

1852 Forced departure from Husum. In the same year a further collection of his poems was published.

1853–64 Service in the Prussian legal administration, first in Potsdam, later in Heiligenstadt.

1864 Return to Husum as *Landvogt*.

1865 Death of his wife Constanze. The following year he married Dorothea Jensen, a childhood friend.

1867 *In St. Jürgen* and *Eine Malerarbeit*.

1871 *Draussen im Heidehof* (story).

1879 Resignation from legal office and retirement to the Holstein village of Hademarschen.

1880–88 Various stories including *Zur Chronik von Grieshuus* (1883) and *Der Schimmelreiter* (1888).

1888 Death of Storm on July 4th: his body was buried in the family grave at Husum.

IMMENSEE

The Old Man

ONE autumn evening an elderly, well-dressed man was
seen coming slowly down the road. To judge from the
dust on his old-fashioned buckled shoes, he was returning from a walk. The joy of his past youth shone in
his dark-brown eyes which contrasted strikingly with
his snow-white hair, and carrying his gold-topped cane
under his arm he looked cheerfully at the surrounding scene and at the town that lay before him in the
glow of the evening sunshine. He almost gave the
impression of being a stranger, for although many of
the passers-by felt drawn to look into his grave eyes,
few exchanged greetings with him.

He stopped at last in front of a house with lofty
gables, gave a final glance down the road and pushed
open the gate that led into the courtyard.

As the bell rang, a green curtain was drawn aside
from a small window overlooking the courtyard, and
an old woman peered out. The old man motioned her
with his cane.

'No lights yet?' he called, in a slightly southern
accent.

The housekeeper lowered the curtain again. He
crossed the broad courtyard, passed through a parlour,
round whose walls stood oak dressers adorned with
china vases, and went through the door opposite into a

small lobby from which a narrow staircase led to the upper rooms at the back of the house.

Climbing the stairs slowly, he opened a door at the top and entered a spacious room. Here everything was quiet and secluded. One wall was almost entirely taken up by shelves and bookcases, while the other was hung with portraits and landscape paintings. A bulky arm-chair with a red velvet cushion was drawn up in front of a green-topped table, on which lay a number of open books.

Putting his hat and cane in a corner, he sat down and folded his hands in front of him as though to rest. It gradually became darker. As he sat there, a ray of moonlight shone through the window, lighting up the paintings, and involuntarily he followed its slow passage across the wall. Then it fell on a small portrait in a simple, black frame.

'Elisabeth!' he whispered. And as he uttered the name, he was transported back to his childhood . . .

The Children

Before long he saw in his mind the figure of a charming young girl come into the room. Her name was Elisabeth, and she must have been about five years old, while he was twice that. Round her neck she wore a red silk scarf that set off her attractive brown eyes.

'Reinhard,' she cried, 'we've got the day off from school, the whole day! And tomorrow as well!'

Reinhard, who already had his slate under his arm, quickly put it down behind the door, and the two children ran through the house into the garden, then out into the fields. The unexpected holiday was just what they wanted, for here Elisabeth had helped Reinhard build a hut out of turfs, in which they were going to spend the summer evenings; the only thing missing was a seat. The nails, the hammer and the planks were already there, so he went straight to work.

In the meantime Elisabeth walked along by the embankment and collected in her apron the ring-shaped seeds of the wild mallow, which they wanted to use for garlands and necklaces. So by the time that Reinhard, despite driving some of the nails in crooked, had finally finished the seat and emerged into the sunshine again, she had reached the far side of the field.

'Elisabeth! Elisabeth!' he shouted. She ran towards him, her hair flying in the wind.

'Come on, our house is ready!' he cried. 'You're hot from running, so let's go and sit on our new seat, and I'll tell you a story.'

They went in and sat down. Taking the ring-like seeds out of her apron, she threaded them on to long strings.

'Once upon a time there were three silk-spinners,' he began.

'But I know that by heart,' interrupted Elisabeth. 'You mustn't keep telling me the same one.'

So Reinhard had to keep the story of the three silk-spinners to himself, and instead he told the story of the poor man who was cast into the lions' den.

'It was night, and pitch black,' he began again, 'and the lions were asleep. From time to time, however, they yawned in their sleep and stretched out their red tongues. When they did this, the poor man trembled and thought that the dawn was at hand. Then suddenly there was a blinding flash, and when he looked up, he saw an angel standing before him. The angel beckoned to him, then vanished into the rock.'

Elisabeth had been listening attentively.

'An angel?' she said. 'Did he have wings?'

'It's only a story,' answered Reinhard. 'Angels don't really exist.'

'What a thing to say!' she exclaimed, looking him straight in the face. But he frowned at her disapprovingly, and in a hesitant voice she asked:

'Then why do people always tell us that they do? Like mother and auntie and the teacher?'

'I don't know,' he replied.

'Do lions really exist, then?'

'Lions? What a question! Of course they do! In India the priests yoke them together in front of their carts and drive through the desert with them. When I grow up, I'm going there to see for myself. It's a thousand times better than here—they haven't any winter. And you must come with me. Will you?'

'Yes,' she replied. 'But my mother must come as well —and yours.'

'No, they can't,' he rejoined. 'They will be too old by then.'

'But I can't come by myself.'

'When the time comes, you will, because you will be my wife, and the others won't have any say in what you do.'

'But my mother would cry.'

'We'll be coming back,' said Reinhard impatiently. 'So tell me straight out: will you come with me? If you won't, I'll go alone. And then I'll never come back.'

Poor Elisabeth was almost in tears.

'Don't look at me so fiercely,' she stammered. 'Of course I'll come.'

Joyfully Reinhard clasped her hands and led her out into the field.

'To India! To India!' he chanted, dancing round and round with her and making her red neckerchief fly out. Suddenly he let go her hands and said gravely:

'It's no good. You're not brave enough.'

'Elisabeth! Reinhard!' came a voice from the garden.

'Here we are!' cried the children, and skipped back to the house hand in hand.

In the Woods

This was the way the two children lived together. Often he found her too quiet, and often she found him too boisterous, but they would not leave each other's side. They spent almost all their free moments together, playing in the cramped confines of their family homes in winter, and outdoors over hill and dale in summer.

Once when Elisabeth received a scolding from the teacher, Reinhard slammed his slate down angrily on his desk to try and attract the teacher's attention to himself. His action passed unnoticed, but he lost all interest in the geography lessons and composed a long poem instead: in it he portrayed himself as a young eagle, the teacher as a black crow and Elisabeth as a white dove, and the eagle vowed to avenge himself on the crow as soon as his wings were fully grown. Tears filled the young poet's eyes, and he saw himself as the instrument of a higher purpose. When he got home, he managed to find a little notebook bound in parchment, and on the opening pages he entered with great care his first poem.

Shortly afterwards he was moved to another school, where he made friends with boys of his own age, but his relationship to Elisabeth remained unaffected. He began to write down some of her favourite tales from among those which he had told and retold in the past. He often felt an urge to add to the stories some ideas of his own but for some reason he found that he could never bring himself to do so. So he copied them just as he had heard them, and when he had finished, he gave them to Elisabeth, who kept them carefully in one of the drawers in her bureau. It gave him a warm feeling of pleasure to listen in the evenings as she read to her mother some of the tales from his manuscript.

Seven years went by, and Reinhard was about to be sent away to complete his education. Elisabeth could not believe there would be a time when there was no Reinhard, and she was happy when he told her one day that he would go on writing down fairy-tales for her as before. He said he would put them in with his letters to his mother, but he wanted her to write and tell him whether she liked them.

As the day of his departure drew near, the number of poems in the little volume grew until it was almost half full. But although the book and most of its poems owed their existence to her, Elisabeth was not admitted into the secret.

It was June. Reinhard was due to leave the next day, and they wanted to have a final celebration together. So it was arranged that there should be a family excursion to the nearby woods.

They drove the hour's journey to the edge of the wood by cart, then took down the hampers and proceeded on foot. First they walked through a cool shady copse of fir trees, where fine needles were strewn everywhere on the ground. Half an hour later they emerged from the darkness of the firs into an open plantation of beech trees where all was green and bright; an occasional ray of sunlight broke through the rich foliage, and above their heads a squirrel leapt from bough to bough.

The group stopped at a spot where the topmost branches of the ancient beeches had intertwined to form a kind of transparent cupola. Elisabeth's mother opened one of the hampers, and an old gentleman assumed charge of the proceedings.

'Gather round, children,' he called out, 'and listen carefully to what I say. Each of you will be given two dry rolls for lunch. We've forgotten to bring the butter, so if you want something to eat with them, you will have to find it yourselves. There are enough strawberries in the woods for those who know where to look, and those who don't will have to eat dry bread. That's the way things are in life. Do you understand?'

'Yes, yes!' they cried.

'All right,' he resumed. 'But I've not finished yet. We older folk have roamed about enough in our time, so we shall stay here under these leafy trees and peel the potatoes and light the fire and prepare the table. At twelve o'clock we shall boil the eggs. In return for this you will give us half your strawberries, so that we can prepare a dessert. Now away with you to the four winds—and don't cheat!'

The children looked at each other rouguishly.

'Just a moment!' called the old man again. 'If you don't find any strawberries, you needn't bring any back —that goes without saying. But nor will you get anything from us—so get that into your pretty little heads! Well, that's enough good advice for one day; if you get some strawberries as well, you'll find your way through life all right.'

The children thought so too, and set off on their journey in pairs.

'Come on, Elisabeth,' said Reinhard. 'I know a strawberry-bed. You won't have to eat dry bread.'

Tying the green ribbons of her straw hat together, she hung it over her arm.

'All right,' she said. 'I've got a basket for them.'

They walked further and further into the wood, past dark, shadowy trees where all was dank and still, the silence broken only by the cry of the hawks, out of sight in the air above them. Then came dense undergrowth, so thick that Reinhard had to go in front to clear a path, breaking down branches and bending creepers aside.

Then he heard Elisabeth calling behind him. He turned round.

'Reinhard,' she cried. 'Wait!'

At first he could not see her. Then he caught sight of her some distance away, fighting to get through the bushes, her little head bobbing about just above the tall ferns around her. Going back, he led her through the tangled undergrowth to a clearing where blue butterflies fluttered among the wild flowers. Reinhard stroked her damp hair from her flushed face and wanted to put the straw hat on her head. At first she resisted, but then he asked her to let him do so, and she finally consented.

'But where are the strawberries you talked about?' she asked, stopping to recover her breath.

'They used to grow here,' he replied, 'but the toads have been here before us, or perhaps it was the martens —or the elves.'

'The leaves are still here,' said Elisabeth, as she looked. 'But don't talk about elves. I'm not a bit tired, so let's look further on.'

There was a little stream in front of them, beyond which the wood continued, and lifting her up, Reinhard carried her across. After a while they came out of the shady forest into a broad clearing.

'There must be strawberries growing here,' said Elisabeth. 'There is such a sweet smell.'

They looked everywhere in the sunlit glade but found none.

'No, it's only the scent of the heather,' said Reinhard at length.

A straggling mass of briars and raspberry bushes surrounded them, and the air was filled with the strong scent of the herbs growing among the short grass.

'How lonely it is here,' said Elisabeth. 'I wonder where the others are?'

Reinhard had forgotten how to get back.

'Wait a moment,' he said. 'Which direction is the wind coming from?' And he held up his hand.

But there was no wind.

'Quiet!' whispered Elisabeth. 'I think I hear voices. Shout to them!'

Cupping his hands round his mouth, Reinhard cried:
'This way!'

And back came the echo: 'This way!'

'They've heard us!' cried Elisabeth, clapping her hands in joy.

'No, it was only an echo.'

Clutching his hand, she stammered:

'I'm frightened!'

'There's no reason to be,' he answered. 'This is a wonderful spot. Sit down on the grass over there, where it's shady. We'll rest a while and then look for the others.'

Elisabeth sat down beneath the spreading branches of a beech tree and strained her ears. Reinhard sat on the stump of a tree a few yards away and looked across at her in silence. The sun stood high in the sky, beating down upon them with the full force of noonday. The air was full of tiny, steel-blue insects, their glittering wings humming and buzzing in the heat, and at times the knocking of the woodpeckers or the screech of other forest birds was heard from the heart of the woods.

'Listen,' said Elisabeth suddenly. 'There's a bell ringing.'

'Where?'

'Behind us. Can't you hear it? It must be midday.'

'Then the town is behind us. If we go straight on in this direction, we're bound to meet the others.'

So they started back, for Elisabeth was tired, and they had given up looking for strawberries. At last they heard the sound of laughter from among the trees. As they approached, they saw a snow-white cloth spread out on the ground to make a table, and on it masses and masses of strawberries. The old gentleman had stuck a serviette in the buttonhole of his waistcoat

and was continuing his moralising discourse to the chil-
ren, busily slicing up the joint as he talked.

'Ah, here come the stragglers!' cried the others, as
they caught sight of Reinhard and Elisabeth through
the trees.

'This way!' called the old man. 'Open your bags and
empty your hats! Let's see what you've found!'

'Only hunger and thirst!' said Reinhard.

'Well, if that's all you've got,' returned the old man,
offering them the well-filled dish, 'you'd better keep
it. You remember the agreement: no food for the idle.'

However, they eventually succeeded in winning him
over, and the meal commenced, while the thrushes sang
merrily in the nearby juniper bushes.

So the day passed. But Reinhard *had* found something. And although it had nothing to do with strawberries, it did owe its life to the woods. When he arrived home in the evening, he took out his old parchment book and wrote:

> Here at the foot of the mountain
>   No raucous wind will blow;
> The verdant branches bow their heads
>   To shield the child below.
>
> She sits upon the scented bank,
>   She breathes a fragrance rare;
> And all the while the insects buzz
>   And chirrup in the air.
>
> The wood is clothed in silence;
>   She sits there so serene,
> While shafts of light caress her hair
>   And bathe it in their sheen.

I hear the cuckoo's happy call,
　And tremble at the thought
That here before me, golden-eyed,
　The Forest Queen holds court.

So she was not only a creature whom he had taken
under his protecting wing: she also symbolised for him
all the delight and glory of his own rise to manhood.

A Child Stood by the Roadside

Christmas Eve arrived. It was still afternoon when
Reinhard sat at the old oak table in the Ratskeller with
a group of his fellow-students. The wall-lamps had
been lit, for down here it was already dark. As
yet, however, only a few guests had assembled, and
the waiters were leaning casually against the pillars. In
one corner of the vaulted room sat a fiddler, and at his
side a girl of gypsy-like appearance who was holding a
zither. They were resting their instruments on their
knees and staring listlessly in front of them.

From the students' table came the pop of a champagne cork.

'Drink up, my Bohemian sweetheart!' cried an aristo-
cratic young dandy, holding out a glass to her.

'I don't want to,' answered the girl, without moving.

'Then sing!' he said, throwing a silver coin into her lap.

Slowly she ran her fingers through her black hair,
and the fiddler whispered something in her ear. But she
tossed her head, rested her chin on her zither and said:

'I'm not going to play for him!'

Jumping up, glass in hand, Reinhard went over to
her.

'And what do you want?' she asked defiantly.

'I want to see your eyes.'

'What have my eyes got to do with you?'

Looking down at her impishly, Reinhard said:

'They have a deceitful expression in them—I can see.'

She leaned her cheek against her hand and looked at him suspiciously. Reinhard raised his glass to his lips and said:

'Here's to your wicked, beautiful eyes!'

Laughingly she threw her head back.

'Give me your glass,' she said, and slowly finished the champagne, keeping her black eyes fixed on him. Then she struck a chord on her zither and sang in a low voice throbbing with emotion:

> 'Today I am happy,
> Today I am gay;
> Tomorrow my laughter
> Will vanish away.
>
> Just for the moment
> I call you my own;
> But at my death
> I shall suffer alone.'

As the fiddler quickly struck up his ritornello, a new-comer joined the group.

'I called for you, Reinhard,' he said, 'but you had already left. Santa Claus had paid you a visit, though.'

'Santa Claus!' laughed Reinhard. 'He doesn't come to me any more!'

'That's where you're wrong! Your room was full of the smell of spice-cake and pine-needles.'

Putting down his glass, Reinhard reached for his cap.

'Where are you going?' asked the girl.

'I'll be back in a while.'

She frowned. 'Stay with me!' she whispered, look-ing at him affectionately.

'I cannot,' he faltered.

She pushed him away with her foot and sneered:

'Go, then! You're no use—just like the rest of them!'

She turned her back on him, and he slowly climbed the stairs and left.

Outside it was getting dark, and he felt the cold win-ter air against his glowing cheeks. Here and there the lighted candles on a Christmas tree shone through the windows, and from time to time he heard the sound of penny whistles and tin trumpets and the ring of happy voices inside. Groups of beggar-children shuffled from house to house or climbed up on to the balustrade to catch a glimpse of the forbidden joys within. Some-times a door was suddenly opened, and harsh voices drove the beggars away from the brightly lit house and out on to the dark alley, while from the porch of a house nearby came the strains of an old carol sung by a party of boys and girls.

But Reinhard did not hear them. He hurried from one street to the next until he reached his house. By this time it was almost completely dark. He stumbled up the stairs and into his room. He was greeted by a sweet scent which reminded him of Christmas with his mother.

Trembling, he lit the lamp. An enormous parcel lay on the table, and when he opened it, the familiar little brown cakes fell out. Some of them were decorated with his initials in coloured sugar dots—no one but Elisabeth could have done that. Then he found a smaller parcel with fine, embroidered shirts, kerchiefs and frills, and finally two letters, one from his mother, the other from Elisabeth. Opening the latter, he read:

The pretty sugar initials will tell you who helped to bake the cakes, and the same person embroidered the frills. Our Christmas Eve will be very quiet. Mother always puts her spinning-wheel away at half-past nine, and this winter it has been very lonely without you. Last Sunday the linnet you gave me died; I cried for a long while, for I always looked after it so well. It used to sing in the afternoons when the sun shone into its cage, and mother used to hang a cloth over it to keep it quiet when it was in full cry.

So now the room is even quieter, though your old friend Erich visits us from time to time. You once said that he looked like the brown overcoat he always wears, and I cannot help thinking of that every time he enters the room—it is really too funny. But please do not say anything to mother, because it might annoy her.

Guess what I am going to give your mother for Christmas! You can't? I'm giving her myself! Erich is drawing a portrait of me in charcoal; I have already sat for him on three occasions—a whole hour each time. I found it very embarrassing to let a stranger get to know my features so closely, and I did not want to do it, but my mother persuaded me to: she said it would give dear Frau Werner such great pleasure.

Reinhard, you have not kept your promise: you have not sent me any fairy-tales. I often complained to your mother, but she always says that you have more important things to think about now—but I think there is another reason.

Then Reinhard read the letter from his mother. When he had finished them both, he folded them up and put them away. An uncontrollable feeling of home-sickness came over him, and he walked up and down in his room, murmuring:

> 'The stranger's path was lonely;
> His steps had led astray;
> A child stood by the roadside
> And motioned him the way.'

He went to his desk, took out some money and went down into the street again. Things had become quieter: the candles on the Christmas trees had gone out and the children's procession had left. As the wind swept through the deserted streets, he saw family groups sitting in their houses, old and young together. The second part of the Christmas Eve celebrations had begun.

As Reinhard approached the Ratskeller, the sound of the violin and the zither-girl's song floated up to him. Then the bell tinkled, a dark figure pushed open the door and stumbled up the broad, dimly lit steps to the pavement. Reinhard moved into the shadows and walked quickly past. A short distance further he came to a brightly lit jeweller's shop; going in, he pawned a little crucifix made of red coral and then went back the same way that he had come.

Near his house he saw a little girl in tattered clothes trying vainly to open the door.

'Shall I help you?' he asked.

The child let go the heavy handle but said nothing. Reinhard opened the door.

'No, don't go in,' he said, 'they might send you away

again. Come with me instead, and I'll give you some Christmas titbits.'

Closing the door again, he took her by the hand, and she walked with him silently to his house.

He had left the light burning when he went out.

'Here are some cakes for you,' he said, tipping half of his precious store into her apron, except for those with the sugar-covered letters.

'Now go home and share them with your mother,' he said.

The child looked shyly up at him as though unaccustomed to such generosity and not knowing what to answer. He opened the door and raised the candle to show her the way. Clasping her treasure, she skipped down the steps and out of the house like a deer.

Reinhard stoked up his stove and put the dusty inkwell on the desk. Then he sat down and began to write, and the whole night he wrote letters to his mother and to Elisabeth. The remainder of the cakes lay untouched beside him; he had, however, buttoned on the frills that Elisabeth had sent him, and they made a strange contrast to his white robe. He was still sitting there when the winter sun rose, casting its rays on to the frozen window-panes and revealing in the mirror on the opposite wall a grim, pale face.

Home

After Easter had passed Reinhard went home, and the morning after his arrival he went to see Elisabeth.

'How you've grown!' he exclaimed, as the slim, attractive young girl came towards him with a smile.

She blushed, but said nothing and tried gently to withdraw her hand, which he was still holding in welcome. He looked at her, puzzled: she had never acted like this before, and he felt as though something had come between them.

And although he came to see her every day, the feeling persisted. There were sometimes embarrassing silences as they sat together, despite his anxious efforts to cover them up. So in order to have some definite plan of activity during his holiday, he began to teach her botany, a subject that he had studied off and on during the early months of his university career. Elisabeth, who was accustomed to following his lead and was, in addition, possessed of a lively intelligence, participated eagerly in the work. Several times a week they made excursions into the nearby heathlands and fields, returning home at noontime with their collecting-box full of plants and blossoms. When Reinhard came back to her house again a few hours later, they shared the treasures between them.

On one such occasion Reinhard arrived to find her standing by the window, draping wisps of chickweed over a gilded bird-cage which he had not seen there before. In the cage sat a canary, fluttering its wings and screeching as it pecked at Elisabeth's fingers. It was here that Reinhard's linnet used to be.

'Did my poor little linnet turn into a goldfinch when he died?' he asked jokingly.

'Linnets do not turn into goldfinches,' answered Elisabeth's mother stiffly, as she sat at her spinning-wheel. 'Elisabeth's friend Erich sent her the bird today from his estate.'

'Which estate?'

'Don't you know?'

'Know what?'

'That Erich took over his father's other estate on Immensee a month ago?'

'But you did not tell me a word about it.'

'Nor did you ask a thing about him. He has developed into a most kind and considerate young man.'

She went out of the room to attend to the coffee. Meanwhile Elisabeth had turned away and was arranging the little bower of chickweed over the cage.

'I shan't be a moment,' she said. 'I've almost finished.'

Contrary to his custom, Reinhard did not reply, and she looked round. There was a sad expression in his eyes such as she had never seen before.

'What is the matter, Reinhard?' she asked, coming over to him.

'The matter?'

He stared into her eyes as though in a daze.

'You look so sad.'

'It's the canary,' he said. 'I cannot bear to see it here.' She looked at him in astonishment.

'How strange you are!' she murmured.

He took her hands and held them gently in his own. A moment later her mother came back into the room.

After coffee Elisabeth's mother returned to her spinning-wheel, while Elisabeth and Reinhard went into the next room to arrange their plants. They counted the stamens, carefully spread out the leaves and the petals, and placed two of each kind between the pages of a thick book to press them. The sun was shining in the stillness of the afternoon; the only sound was the whirr of the spinning-wheel in the adjoining room, or Reinhard's subdued tones as he enumerated the classes and species of the plants and corrected Elisabeth's hesitant pronunciation of their Latin names.

'I cannot find the lily of the valley we brought home the other day,' she said, after they had arranged the whole collection.

Reinhard pulled a small white book, bound in parchment, out of his pocket.

'Here is one for you,' he said, taking a half-dried flower from between the pages.

Elisabeth recognised his writing in the book.

'Have you been composing fairy-stories again?' she asked.

'Not fairy-stories,' he replied, handing her the book.

It was full of poems, most of them not more than one page long. Elisabeth looked through them, apparently reading only the titles: 'The Time She Was Scolded by the Teacher'; 'The Time They Lost Their Way in the Forest'; 'The Easter Tale'; 'The First Time She Wrote to Me'—almost all of them were in this vein.

Reinhard watched her attentively and observed that, as she turned the pages, a delicate flush came to her fair cheeks and spread over her face. He tried to look into her eyes but she would not raise her head. Finally she put the book down without saying a word.

'Don't give it back to me just like that!' he said.

She took a brown sprig from the collecting-box.

'I've put your favourite leaf inside it,' she said, and handed the book back to him.

The vacation was over and the day of Reinhard's departure had arrived. At her request Elisabeth was allowed to accompany him to the stage-coach, which left from a few streets away. As they went out of the house, Reinhard offered the slender young girl his arm, and the two walked silently side by side. The nearer they came to the coach-stop, the more urgently did Reinhard feel that there was something he had to tell her before he went away for such a long time, something on which the whole value and enjoyment of his future life depended. Yet he could not find the words that would relieve his mind of its burden, and in his despondency he began to walk more and more slowly.

'You will be late,' she said. 'The clock on the Marien-kirche has already struck ten.'

But this did not make him walk any faster. At last he stammered:

'Elisabeth, we shall not see each other for two years. Will you be as fond of me when I come back as you are now?'

She nodded her head and looked kindly at him. There was a pause. Then she said:

'I defended you, too.'

'Defended me? Against whom?'

'My mother. We talked about you for a long time yesterday evening after you had left. She said you were not as affectionate as you used to be.'

Reinhard was silent for a moment. Then taking her hand and gazing earnestly into her childlike eyes, he said:

'I am as affectionate as I always was. You do believe that, Elisabeth, don't you?'

'Yes,' she replied.

He let go her hand, and they walked rapidly down the last street. The closer the moment of departure

came, the happier his expression grew, and she could
scarcely keep up with him.

'What is the matter, Reinhard?' she asked.

'I have a wonderful secret,' he said, looking at her
in radiant happiness. 'I'll tell you what it is in two
years' time, when I come back."

They had reached the coach, which was still waiting
there. Taking her hand for the last time, he said:

'Good-bye, Elisabeth! Don't forget what I told you!'

She shook her head.

'Good-bye,' she echoed.

He got into the coach and the horses galloped away.
As it went round the corner, he caught a final glimpse
of her walking slowly back along the road.

A Letter

Almost two years had passed. Reinhard was sitting
at his desk between piles of books and papers, waiting
for a friend who used to come and study with him.
He heard footsteps ascending the stairs.

'Come in!' he called out.

It was his landlady.

'A letter for you, Herr Werner,' she said. She handed
it to him and went out.

Since his last visit home Reinhard had neither written to Elisabeth nor received any letters from her. And
this was not from her either, but from his mother. He
opened it and began to read. Then he came to this
passage:

> 'When one is at your age, my son, each year
> seems to take on a different appearance. Youth is

always looking for new fields to conquer. Here at home certain things have happened which, if I understand your mood aright, may at first bring you grief. Yesterday Elisabeth finally consented to marry Erich, who had twice asked for her hand in the past three months. Although on these occasions she had not been able to bring herself to accept him, this time she has finally made her decision—young though she is. The wedding is to take place shortly, and they will then leave here, together with her mother.'

Immensee

The years went by. One warm spring afternoon a sturdy young man with sun-tanned features was striding along a shady woodland track that led down the hillside. His grey eyes gazed searchingly into the distance, as though he expected the path to change its course at some point, but it never did.

A horse and cart came into view, moving slowly up the slope.

'Good-day, friend!' the man called out to the farmer who was walking at the side of the cart. 'Is this the way to Immensee?'

'Straight on,' answered the farmer, touching his cap.

'Is it far?'

'You're almost there. Before you've smoked half a pipeful of tobacco, you'll see the lake. The house is close by.'

The farmer trudged onwards, while the young man quickened his pace as he passed beneath the trees.

A quarter of an hour later the woods on his left came

abruptly to an end, and the track led past a steep slope from the bottom of which oak trees a hundred years old and more stretched upwards, almost reaching the path with their topmost branches. A sunlit landscape stretched into the distance beyond the trees, and in the depths below nestled the lake, its tranquil, deep-blue waters almost completely surrounded with bright green woodlands, which parted at a single point to allow a glimpse of the hazy blue mountains that dominated the horizon. On the other side, amid the green foliage of the forest, stood fruit trees in full bloom, their white blossom gleaming like a carpet of snow, and from their midst emerged the white house with its red tiled roof.

A stork flew up from the chimney and circled slowly above the lake.

'Immensee!' cried the traveller.

He felt as though he had already reached his journey's end. He stood still for a moment, looking out across the trees below him towards the other side of the lake, where the gentle ripples caught the reflection of the house. Then he walked quickly on.

The path led steeply down the mountainside. He was now in the shade of the trees again, but the lake was hidden to open view and its shining waters were only visible for seconds between the swaying branches. After a while the track began to climb again, and the trees on both sides stopped; in their place grew thick vines, behind which stood an orchard of fruit trees, where the bees buzzed happily from blossom to blossom.

A distinguished-looking man in a brown cloak came towards the traveller. As he reached him, he swung his cap in the air and cried joyously:

'Welcome, Brother Reinhard! Welcome to Immensee!"

'God's blessing on you, Erich—and my thanks for your welcome!'

The two men shook each other warmly by the hand.

'Is it really you?' exclaimed Erich, looking closely at his friend's grave features.

'Of course it is! And it's really you, too—though you seem to look happier than you ever did before.'

A smile of pleasure crossed Erich's face, making his homely features look even more cheerful.

'Well,' he said, shaking Reinhard's hand again, 'fortune has smiled on me since then, as you know.'

He rubbed his hands in delight and cried:

'What a surprise! You are the last person she expects to see!'

'A surprise for whom?' asked Reinhard.

'For Elisabeth!'

'But did you not tell her I was coming?'

'Not a word. She has no idea, nor has her mother. I kept it to myself so that they would be all the more delighted. I always had secret plans for this.'

As they came nearer the house, Reinhard lapsed into silence. A constricting hand seemed to stifle his breath.

On the left side of the path the vines now gave way to an extensive kitchen-garden which stretched down almost to the lakeside. The stork was now strutting solemnly to and fro between the vegetable beds.

'Off with you!' shouted Erich, clapping his hands. 'Just look at that lanky Egyptian eating my pea-shoots!'

The bird slowly raised its neck and then flew off to the end of the garden, perching on the roof of a new building against whose walls peach and apricot trees were growing in a criss-cross pattern.

'That's the distillery,' said Erich. 'I only put it up two years ago. My grandfather built the living quarters, and my late father had the farm buildings renovated. So, step by step, new things get done.'

They came to a broad courtyard enclosed by the farm buildings at the sides and the family mansion at the rear. Built on to the two wings of the mansion was a high wall behind which could be seen the dark outline of yew hedges, while occasional lilac bushes cast their blossoms over the courtyard itself. Sun-tanned men, their faces bathed in perspiration, bade the two friends good-day as they walked past and Erich called out to them to enquire about the day's work or to give them fresh instructions.

They reached the mansion and entered a cool, lofty hallway, from the end of which a dark corridor branched off to the left. Erich opened a door, and they passed into a spacious drawing-room which led into the garden. The sun shone through the thick foliage that hung down in front of the windows, bathing the walls in a green glow, while the centre of the room was illuminated by the full glory of the spring sunlight as it poured through the tall French windows, which stood wide open. Beyond the windows was a view of the garden with its round flower-beds and its tall hedgerows. A broad, straight path ran right through the centre of the garden, and by looking down it, one could see the lake and the forest beyond. A wave of perfume greeted the friends as they entered.

On the terrace sat a girl-like figure, dressed in white. As the two men entered the room, she rose from her

seat and walked towards them. Suddenly she stopped
as though rooted to the spot, and stared at the stranger.
Smilingly he stretched out his hands towards her.

'Reinhard!' she cried. 'Reinhard! Can it really be
you? It is years since we last saw each other!'

'Years!' he repeated. His voice faltered and he could
not go on. The sound of her voice pierced his heart,
and when he raised his eyes, he saw her standing before
him, the same slim, delicate creature to whom he had
said good-bye years ago in his home town.

Beaming with pleasure, Erich watched from the door.

'Well, Elisabeth,' he said, 'this was the last person
you expected to see, was it not?'

She looked at him with the affection of a sister.

'How kind you are, Erich!' she said.

He took her delicate hand in his and caressed it.

'And now that he is here,' he continued, 'we shall not
let him go in a hurry. He has been roaming the world
long enough, and we are going to make him feel at
home again. Look what a foreign and distinguished
appearance he has acquired!'

Elisabeth glanced shyly at Reinhard.

'He only looks like that because we have not seen
him for so long,' she said.

At that moment her mother entered, carrying a basket on her arm. Catching sight of Reinhard, she exclaimed:

'Well, well! Herr Werner! An unexpected but ever
welcome guest!'

And then the conversation began to flow back and
forth. The women sat down at their needlework, and
while Reinhard partook of the refreshments that had
been prepared for him, Erich lit his massive meerschaum

and puffed away as he sat talking at Reinhard's side.

The next day Reinhard was made to accompany Erich on a tour of inspection of the fields, the vineyards, the hop-gardens and the distillery. Everything was in perfect repair; the workers, both those in the fields and those in the distillery, looked healthy and contented.

At noon the family met in the drawing-room and spent as much of the remainder of the day together as their free time allowed. The hours before the evening meal, like those at the very beginning of the day, Reinhard spent working in his room. For years he had been collecting folk-songs and rhymes, wherever he could find them; he was now engaged in arranging his collection, and hoped to add some items to it from the neighbourhood.

Elisabeth was at all times kind and gentle. She accepted Erich's attentions with almost humble gratitude, and Reinhard could not resist the thought that the vivacious friend of his childhood had seemed likely to grow into a less sedate person than the woman he now saw before him.

Since his second day in Erich's house Reinhard had made it a habit to take an evening stroll by the lake shore. The path led close by the garden, and at the end of it, on a raised promontory and overhung with tall birches, stood a bench. Elisabeth's mother had christened it the 'evening bench', because it faced the setting sun, and because it was in the evening that the family usually sat there.

One evening Reinhard was returning from his walk along this path when it began to rain. He tried to shel-

ter beneath a linden-tree which stood at the water's
edge, but soon the heavy raindrops started to come
through the leaves. He was already soaked to the skin,
so he resigned himself to the situation and resumed
his homeward trek.

The rain became heavier, and it was almost dark. As
he came near to the 'evening bench', he imagined that
he saw a woman dressed in white standing motionless
beneath the glistening birch trees, facing in his direction as though expecting someone to pass. Her features
seemed like those of Elisabeth. He hastened his steps,
but as he made to approach her and accompany her
back to the house, she turned slowly away and vanished
along the dark paths at the side.

He was baffled, and almost felt a surge of resentment
against Elisabeth, but he could not be certain that it
had really been she whom he had seen. Yet he was reluctant to ask her, and when he got back to the house,
he did not go into the drawing-room for fear she might
come in through the French windows.

My Mother wished it So

A few evenings later the family were sitting together
in the drawing-room as usual. The windows were open
and the sun had already sunk behind the trees on the
far side of the lake.

They asked Reinhard to let them hear some of the
folk-songs which a friend living in the country had
sent him that afternoon. He went up to his room and
returned with a sheaf of papers covered with fine hand-
writing.

They sat down at the table, Reinhard next to Elisabeth.

'We must hope for the best,' he said. 'I have not yet looked through them myself.'

Elisabeth unrolled the manuscript.

'There is music as well,' she said. 'You must sing it to us, Reinhard.'

He read out a few Tyrolese *Schnaderhüpferl*,[1] casually interspersing a few snatches of the cheerful melody. A happy mood settled over the little group.

'Who composed such pretty songs?' asked Elisabeth.

'That's easy to guess,' said Erich: 'barbers, tailors' apprentices and other lighthearted folk.'

'But they are not composed,' said Reinhard, 'they just grow, or fall from the sky, and spread hither and thither over the countryside like gossamer. People sing them in a thousand different places at the same time, expressing in them man's most personal thoughts and deeds. It is as though we have all taken part in their making.'

Picking up another, he read:

'I stood upon a mountain-top . . .'

'I know that one!' cried Elisabeth. 'Come on, Reinhard, I'll sing it with you!'

And together, Elisabeth singing the descant in her soft contralto voice, they sang that melody which sounds so mysterious that it seems hardly to be the creation of human minds.

Elisabeth's mother was busy with her needlework, while Erich folded his hands and listened devotedly.

[1] Yodelling songs.

When they had finished, Reinhard put the music away
without a word.

The sound of cow-bells floated up from the lake-
shore on the stillness of the evening air, and as they
listened they heard the ringing tones of a boy's voice:

> 'I stood upon a mountain-top
> And saw the depths below . . .'

'You see?' smiled Reinhard as he listened. 'These
songs live on.'

'We often hear singing in these parts,' said Elisabeth.

'It's the boy driving the cattle home,' added Erich.

They listened until the sound of the bells finally died
away behind the farm buildings on the hillside.

'Those are the sounds of primeval nature,' said Reinhard. 'They come from the depths of the earth, and
no one knows who invented them.'

He picked out another sheet from the pile.

The sun was setting, and a hazy red glow settled over
the woods beyond the lake. Reinhard unrolled the
manuscript. Elisabeth held one side of it in her hand,
and they looked at it together as Reinhard read:

> 'My mother wished it so,
> Yet it was not my will
> That I should leave the love I had,
> Surrender to another lad,
> And bid my heart be still.
>
> My mother bears the blame
> For my unhappy state:
> The things that should bring joy in life
> Have nurtured shame and guilt and strife—
> But now it is too late.

All pride and joy is gone,
And anguish fills my mind.
Would that I could forget my pain,
Could wander through the world again
And leave my cares behind!'

Reinhard felt the sheet tremble as he read, and when he had finished, Elisabeth rose from her chair and went out silently into the garden, watched by her mother. Erich was on the point of following her, but her mother held him back.

'Elisabeth has some things to attend to outside,' she said. So he let her go.

Outside the darkness was closing in around the lake and the garden, moths fluttered past the open doors through which the scent of flowers and bushes was wafted in; from the water came the sound of the croaking of frogs, and as the moon rose, the song of nightingales was heard, one from beneath the windows and another in the distance. For a long while he stared at the bushes through which the frail figure of Elisabeth had passed, then rolled up his manuscript, took his leave of the others and left the house in the direction of the lake.

The woods were silent, casting their dark shadow far out over the water, while the centre of the lake was illuminated by the pale moonlight. From time to time the leaves rustled, but there was no wind—only the gentle breath of the mild summer night.

Reinhard walked by the side of the water. Within a stone's throw of the bank he caught sight of a white water-lily and suddenly felt an urge to see it from close quarters.

Taking off his clothes, he entered the water. Plants

and sharp stones stung his feet, and it was too shallow
to swim. Then suddenly the ground sloped away; the
waters swirled over his head, and it took him some time
to fight his way to the surface.

He swam around a little until he had gained his bear-
ings, then, catching a glimpse of the lily as it lay between
the broad, shining leaves, he swam out slowly towards
it, the moonlight shining on the drops of water that
fell from his glistening arms as he propelled himself
forwards. But the distance between him and the lily
never seemed to change, whilst the bank behind him
became more and more indistinct. Yet he had no
thought of turning back, and swam with powerful
strokes towards the middle.

At length he came close enough to the flower to be
able to distinguish its silver leaves in the moonlight,
but as he did so, he felt as though he were becoming
entangled in a net: the smooth stems stretched up from
the bottom of the lake and twined themselves around
his naked limbs. The black waters swirled around mys-
teriously, and he heard a fish leap up behind him. In a
fit of panic he tore the clinging tendrils savagely from
his body and struck out feverishly for the bank. When
he finally reached it and looked back across the water,
the lily was still floating there above the distant murky
depths.

He put on his clothes and walked slowly homewards.
As he entered the drawing-room from the garden, he
found Erich and Elisabeth's mother making arrange-
ments for a short business trip the following day.

'Where have you been at this time of the night?' she
cried as she caught sight of Reinhard.

'Where have I been?' he repeated. 'Why, I wanted to

visit the water-lily, but I found that it could not be done.'

'Who can be expected to believe that?' said Erich. 'How in Heaven's name can one visit a water-lily?'

'I once knew her,' answered Reinhard, 'but that was a long while ago.'

Elisabeth

The following afternoon Reinhard and Elisabeth went for a stroll on the far side of the lake, sometimes passing through wooded copses, sometimes walking along the raised bank by the water's edge. Erich had told Elisabeth that, while her mother and he were away, she should show Reinhard the most attractive views of the surrounding landscape, in particular those of the house itself from the other side of the lake.

They walked from one place to another. At last Elisabeth became tired; she sat down in the shade of the overhanging branches, while Reinhard leaned against a tree opposite her. A cuckoo called from the depths of the forest—and suddenly he had the feeling that he had lived this scene before. Looking at her with a strange smile, he said :

'Shall we go and look for strawberries?'

'This is not the season for strawberries,' she replied.

'But it soon will be.'

Elisabeth shook her head without speaking. Then she stood up, and they walked on. Time and again he glanced at the figure tripping gracefully at his side as though she were borne along by her clothes, and often he held back so as to look deep into her eyes.

They came to a grass-covered clearing from which they could see far out into the countryside. Reinhard bent down and picked some of the plants that were growing there. When he looked up, he showed pain and anguish in his face.

'Do you recognise this flower?' he murmured.

She looked at him in surprise.

'It's heather. I've often picked it in the woods.'

'I have an old book at home,' he said, 'in which, a long while ago, I used to write down all kinds of poems and rhymes. There is heather—a faded one—pressed between its pages. Do you know who gave it to me?'

She nodded silently, casting her eyes down and looking only at the little flower that he held in his hand. For a long time they stood there, motionless. When at last she raised her head, he saw that her eyes were filled with tears.

'Our childhood lies beyond those mountains, Elisabeth,' he said softly. 'What has happened to it?'

They both fell silent and walked on side by side towards the lake. The air was humid, and dark clouds were gathering in the west.

'There's going to be a storm,' said Elisabeth, quickening her step.

Reinhard nodded. They hurried along the bank until they reached the spot where they had left their boat.

As Reinhard pulled at the oars, she let her hand rest on the side of the boat. He looked towards her, but she stared past him into the distance. He lowered his gaze, and his eyes came to rest on her hand. This pale hand, resting on the boat, told him all that her face had withheld from him; subtly but plainly it betrayed, as a beautiful hand so often will, the heart that suffers

secretly in the loneliness of the night. When she noticed
him looking at it, she let it slip slowly over the side
of the boat into the water.

As they walked up to the house, they saw a knife-
grinder's cart. A man with long black hair was busily
operating the treadle, humming a gypsy song as he did
so, while his dog, chained to the cart, slept by his side.
At the entrance to the yard stood a tattered beggar-
girl with fine but haggard features, who stretched out
her hand imploringly to Elisabeth.

Reinhard put his hand in his pocket, but before he
could find something to give her, Elisabeth hastily
emptied the entire contents of her purse into the beg-
gar-girl's hand. Then she turned away abruptly, and
Reinhard heard her sobbing as she went up the steps
into the house. He wanted to stop her, then changed his
mind and stayed at the foot of the steps. The beggar-
girl was still standing there, motionless, clasping the
money in her hands.

'What else do you want?' demanded Reinhard.

She gave a start.

'Nothing,' she stammered, and walked slowly towards the gate, staring back at him with her fiery
eyes as she went. He shouted something at her but she
was out of earshot, and with bowed head, her arms
folded, she passed out of the yard.

> But at my death
> I shall suffer alone.

The strains of the old song sounded in his ears, and his
heart stood still. Then he turned away and went up to
his room.

He sat down and tried to work, but his mind was

a blank and after half-an-hour's fruitless effort he went
down into the drawing-room. The room was empty;
only the evening sunlight shone in through the overhanging foliage. On Elisabeth's bureau there lay a red
scarf that she had been wearing that afternoon. He
picked it up, but it hurt his hand and he put it back
quickly.

Seized by a sudden restlessness, he left the house and
went down to the lake. Untying the boat, he rowed
over to the other side and retraced all the paths along
which he had walked with Elisabeth earlier in the day.

By the time he got back, it was dark. Elisabeth's
mother and Erich had just returned, and as he crossed
the courtyard, the coachman passed him, leading the
horses out to graze. Entering the hall, he heard Erich
walking up and down in the drawing-room; he did not
go in but paused for a moment, then went quietly up
the stairs to his room.

He sat down in the armchair by the window and
tried to listen to the throbbing music of the nightingale
in the hedges below. But all he could hear was the beat
of his own heart. Everybody else in the house had gone
to bed.

The night wore on, and still he sat there. At last,
hours later, he rose from the chair and lay down in
front of the open window. The dew had settled on the
leaves, and the nightingale was no longer singing.
Slowly the deep blue of the night sky gave way to a
pale yellow glow from the east, and a cold breeze
caressed his fevered brow. The first lark flew upwards,
singing joyously.

Reinhard turned away abruptly and walked across
to his desk. He felt for a pencil, sat down and wrote a

few lines on a sheet of paper. Then leaving the paper on the desk, he got up, took his hat and cane, opened the door softly and went downstairs.

Everything was still. The big cat stretched itself on the mat and arched its back as he bent down to stroke it. In the garden the sparrows were proclaiming to all and sundry that the night was past.

He heard a door open and the sound of footsteps on the stairs. Looking up, he found Elisabeth standing in front of him. She put her hand on his arm and her lips moved, but no sound came from them. At last she said:

'Do not deceive me, Reinhard. I know you will never come back.'

'Never,' he repeated.

She drew her hand away and was silent. He walked across the yard towards the gate, then stopped and looked back. She was standing motionless at the same spot, staring blankly after him. He took a step forward and stretched out his arms towards her. Then he turned quickly on his heel and went out of the gate.

Outside the world was bathed in the glow of morning, and the dewdrops in the spiders' webs glistened in the early sunlight.

He did not look back. As he walked swiftly on, the house and the farm buildings grew smaller and smaller, while before him stretched the great wide world . . .

The Old Man

The moon was no longer shining through the window and it had become dark. But still the old man sat in his chair, his hands folded in front of him, and gazed across the room. As he looked, the darkness slowly gave way to the dark waters of a lake; it grew gradually wider and deeper, and at its farthest point, so distant that he could barely see it, there floated a solitary white water-lily, nestling between broad green leaves.

The door opened and a bright ray of light shone into the room.

'I am glad you have come, Brigitte,' he said. 'Put the lamp on the table.'

Then he drew up his chair to the table, picked up one of the open books and engrossed himself in subjects to which he had devoted himself in the days of his youth.

LENZ

GEORG BÜCHNER

Translated by Michael Hamburger

INTRODUCTION

LENZ is the only story known to have been written by
Georg Büchner, the author of *Danton's Death* and
Woyzeck. The story is based on factual evidence.
Büchner's sources were a diary kept by Oberlin in 1778
and a French biography of Oberlin, both of which were
published by friends of Büchner's in 1831.

Though *Lenz* was left unfinished when Büchner died
in 1837—at the age of twenty-three—he wrote it in
Strasbourg in 1836, certainly before *Woyzeck*, possibly
before *Leonce und Lena*. Apart from a single gap which
we can fill in from Büchner's sources, it is unlikely that
he would have substantially changed or amended this
story. The unusual narrative style, with its repetitions,
ellipses and colloquialisms, is wholly in accordance with
his general principles and with the peculiar subject of
this story, a subject wholly beyond the scope of contemporary writers of fiction. Among other things,
Büchner was a brilliant scientist; but his interest in Lenz
was not so much scientific as sympathetic. The aesthetic
principles of Lenz—and other writers of the *Sturm und
Drang* school—link up with Büchner's own innova-
tions, but especially with his creation of a poetic realism
which combines the accurate documentation of facts
with an imaginative interpretation of character. The
aesthetic theories propounded by the Lenz of Büchner's
story are adapted from the theoretical writings of Lenz
himself, such as the following from his *Anmerkungen
zum Theater*: '. . . But since the world has no bridges

and we have to content ourselves with the things that
are there, we do at least feel an accretion to our existence, happiness, by re-creating its Creation on a small
scale.' Büchner's Lenz says almost the same thing in
slightly different words: 'I take it that God has made
the world as it should be ... our only aspiration should
be to re-create modestly in His manner.' Büchner ap-
plied the same principle to *Lenz;* but in spite of his
modest ambition to re-create, rather than to invent, he
invariably improved on his material.

Jacob Michael Reinhold Lenz, the subject of this
story, was born in 1751 in the Baltic province of Livonia.
His father was a Lutheran pastor, and he himself studied
theology at Königsberg. After two years of rather luke-
warm study, he gave up to become private tutor to
the two young Barons von Kleist. In 1771 he travelled
with them to Strasbourg, where he met Goethe. When
Goethe left for a journey with one of the Kleist bro-
thers, Lenz was introduced to Friederike Brion,
Goethe's friend and fell in love with her. He became
notorious as 'Goethe's ape'.

Five years later, in March 1776, he arrived in Weimar,
where Goethe had now settled. Goethe did his best to
be kind to him, but Lenz behaved so eccentrically that
he was asked to leave in December of that year. He
then visited Goethe's brother-in-law at Emmendingen,
moved on to Colmar, where he stayed with G. C.
Pfeffel, and then to Switzerland. There he stayed with
Christoph Kaufmann from November 1777 to January
1778, and suffered his first attack of insanity. Kaufmann
sent him to Oberlin's vicarage in the Steintal and later
visited him there with Lisette Ziegler, his fiancée. This
is the period of Büchner's story. Although Lenz's men-

tal state gradually improved after his removal to Strasbourg, he was taken back to Lithuania in 1779, fell into obscurity and died near Moscow in 1792.

Büchner's material provided him with all the facts and some of the circumstances; but all the descriptions of landscapes—landscapes seen through the eyes of Lenz—and of Lenz's thoughts and feelings are Büchner's contribution. This synthesis of fact and imagination is characteristic of Büchner's work; for he hated Idealism in philosophy and Romanticism in literature. His alternative to these two dominant trends of his time was so disturbingly individual that his works were not appreciated until more than half a century after his death. Since then they have been admired by writers of every school, from the Naturalists to the Symbolists and Expressionists. Some of the finest German prose of this century—such as Hofmannsthal's *Andreas* fragment—shows the unmistakable influence of *Lenz*.

M. H.

PRINCIPAL DATES IN THE LIFE OF
GEORG BÜCHNER

1813 Born on October 17th at Goddelau near Darmstadt, the son of a doctor.

1831 Matriculated as a medical student from Strasbourg University and moved to the University of Giessen.

1833 Secret engagement to Minna Jaeglé, daughter of his landlord in Strasbourg.

1834 Ill with menengitis and went home to recuperate. Began revolutionary activities in a Society for Human Rights. Wrote revolutionary pamphlet *Der Hessische Landbote* with Pastor W. L. Weidig. This pamphlet was seized by the government and his fellow revolutionaries were arrested. Pastor Weidig was tortured and committed suicide.

1835 Wrote *Dantons Tod* to raise money for his flight to Strasbourg where he fled without his father's knowledge. A warrant was issued for his arrest. Lost interest in active politics. Translated *Lucrèce* and *Marie Tudor* by Victor Hugo. Wrote *Lenz*.

1836 Presented his thesis on the nervous system of the barbel to the *Société d'Histoire Naturelle* and was awarded his doctorate. Wrote *Leonce und Lena*. Moved to Zurich and became a lecturer on the comparative anatomy of fishes and amphibia. Probably wrote *Woyzeck* at the end of the year.

1837 Died February 19th of typhus aged twenty-three.

1850 Edition of his works.

1879 Edition of his works.

1902 First performance of *Dantons Tod*.

1911 First performance of *Leonce und Lena*.

1913 First performance of *Woyzeck*.

One other play, *Pietro Aretino*, has been lost, probably destroyed by his fiancée after his death.

LENZ

On the 20th of January Lenz went across the mountains. The summits and the high slopes covered with snow, grey stones all the way down to the valleys, green plains, rocks and pine trees.

It was damp and cold; water trickled down the rocks and gushed over the path. The branches of the pine trees drooped heavily in the moist air. Grey clouds travelled in the sky, but all was so dense—and then the mist rose like steam, slow and clammy, climbed through the shrubs, so lazy, so awkward. Indifferently he moved on; the way did not matter to him, up or down. He felt no tiredness, only sometimes it struck him as unpleasant that he could not walk on his head.

At first there was an urge, a movement inside him, when the stones and rocks bounded away, when the grey forest shook itself beneath him and the mist now blurred its outlines, now half unveiled the trees' gigantic limbs; there was an urge, a movement inside him, he looked for something, as though for lost dreams, but he found nothing. All seemed so small to him, so near, so wet. He would have liked to put the whole earth to dry behind the stove, he could not understand why so much time was needed to descend a steep slope, to reach a distant point; he thought that a few paces should be enough to cover any distance. Only from time to time, when the storm thrust clouds into the valley, and the mist rose in the forest, when the voices near the

rocks awoke, now like thunder subsiding far away,
now rushing back towards him, as if in their wild rejoicing they desired to sing the praise of earth, and
the clouds like wild neighing horses galloped towards
him, and the sunshine pierced in between and came to
draw a flashing sword against the snow-covered plains,
so that a bright, dazzling light cut across the summits
into the valleys; or when the gale drove the clouds
downwards and hurled them into a pale-blue lake, and
then the wind died down and from the depths of the
ravines, from the crests of the pine trees drifted upwards, with a humming like that of lullabies and pealing
bells, and a soft red hue mingled with the deep azure,
and little clouds on silver wings passed across, and everywhere the mountain tops, sharp and solid, shone and
glittered for miles—then he felt a strain in his chest, he
stood struggling for breath, heaving, his body bent forward, his eyes and mouth wide open; he thought that
he must draw the storm into himself, contain it all within him, he stretched himself out and lay on the earth,
dug his way into the All, it was an ecstasy that hurt him
—he rested and laid his head into the moss and half-
closed his eyes, and then it withdrew, away, far away
from him, the earth receded from him, became
small as a wandering star and dipped down into a roar-
ing stream which moved its clear waters beneath him.
But these were only moments; then, soberly, he would
rise, resolute, calm, as though a shadow play had passed
before his eyes—he remembered nothing.

Towards evening he came to the highest point of the
mountain range, to the snow field from which one
descended again into the flat country in the west; he
sat down on the top. It had grown calmer towards

evening; the cloud formations, constant and motionless, hung in the sky; as far as the eyes could reach,
nothing but summits from which broad stretches of
land descended, and everything so still, so grey, lost
in twilight. He experienced a feeling of terrible loneliness; he was alone, quite alone. He wanted to talk to
himself, but he could not, he hardly dared to breathe;
the bending of his feet sounded like thunder beneath
him, he had to sit down. He was seized with a nameless
terror in this nothingness: he was in the void! He
leapt to his feet and rushed down the slope.

It had grown dark, heaven and earth were melting
into one. It seemed as though something were following him, as though something horrible must catch up
with him, something that men cannot bear, as though
madness on horseback were chasing him.

At last he heard voices; he was relieved, his heart
grew lighter. He was told that another half-hour
would see him to Waldbach.

He passed through the village. Lights shone in the
windows, he looked inside as he went by: children at
table, old women, girls, all with quiet, composed faces.
It seemed to him that it was these faces that radiated
light; he began to feel quite cheerful, and soon he was
at the vicarage in Waldbach.

They were at table when he came in; his blond hair
hung in locks about his pale face, his eyes and the cor-
ners of his mouth were twitching, his clothes were
torn.

Oberlin welcomed him, thinking he was a workman:
'You're welcome, although you're a stranger to
me.'

'I'm a friend of——'s, and convey his regards to you.'

'Your name, if you please?'

'Lenz.'

'Ha, ha, ha, has it not appeared in print? Haven't I read several dramas ascribed to a gentleman of that name?'

'Yes, but be kind enough not to judge me by them.'

The conversation continued, he groped for words and told his story quickly, but in torment; gradually he was calmed by the homely room and the quiet faces that stood out from the shadows; the bright child's face on which the light seemed to rest and which looked up inquisitively and trustingly, and the mother who sat further back in the shadow, motionless as an angel. He began to tell them about his home; he drew a number of costumes; they surrounded him closely, sympathetically, soon he felt at home. His pale childish face, now smiling, his lively manner when telling his story! He became calm; it seemed to him as though familiar figures, forgotten faces stepped again from the darkness, old songs awoke, he was away, far away.

At last it was time to go. He was escorted across the street, the vicarage was too small, he was given a room in the schoolhouse. He went upstairs. It was cold up there, a large room, empty, a high bedstead in the background. He put down the light on the table and walked about. He recalled what day it was, how he had come, where he was. The room in the vicarage with its lights, its dear faces; it was like a shadow to him, a dream, and he felt the emptiness again, as he had felt it on the mountain; but now he could not fill it in with anything, the light had gone out, darkness swallowed everything. An unspeakable terror possessed him. He leapt to his feet, ran out of the room, down the stairs, out of the house; but in vain, all was dark, a nothing —even to himself he was a dream. Single, isolated thoughts flickered up, he held them fast; he felt constrained to say 'Our Father' again and again. He could no longer find himself. An obscure instinct urged him to save himself; he ran into stones, tore himself with his nails. The pain began to recall him to consciousness; he hurled himself into the well but the water was not deep, he splashed about.

Then people came; they had heard him, they called out to him. Oberlin came running out. Lenz had come to his senses, the full consciousness of his situation returned to him, he felt more at ease. Now he was ashamed of himself and regretted that he had frightened the good people; he told them it was his habit to take a cold bath, and went back to his room. At last exhaustion gave him rest.

The next day all went well. With Oberlin through the valley on horseback; vast mountain slopes contracting from great heights into a narrow winding valley that extended high up into the mountains in many directions; large masses of rock, which grew wider at the base, very little wooded country, but all rising solemn and grey; a view of the west, into the country and the mountain range that runs from south to north with mighty peaks that stand grave or silently motionless, like a dawning dream. Immense masses of light swelling forth from the valleys at times like a river of gold, and again clouds that hung besides the highest summits and then drifted slowly down the forest into the valley, or rose and sank in shafts of sunlight like a hovering, silvery spectre; no noise, no movement, not a bird, nothing but the now near, now distant flight of the wind. Also there appeared dots, skeletons of huts, boards covered with straw, black, earnest in colour. The people, taciturn and grave, as though afraid to disturb the quiet of their valley, greeted them calmly as they rode by.

Inside the cottages it was lively; everyone crowded around Oberlin, who instructed, advised, consoled; trusting glances, prayers everywhere. The people told of dreams, premonitions. Then quickly returned to practical life; paths constructed, channels dug, school attended. Oberlin was indefatigable, Lenz constantly at his side, conversing, attending to business or submerged in the scenery. All of it had a beneficent, soothing effect upon him. Often he was compelled to look into Oberlin's eyes, and the immense repose communicated to us by nature at rest, in the midst of a forest, in moonlit, melting summer nights, seemed even nearer to him in those calm eyes, those revered, earnest features. He was shy; but he made remarks, he spoke. To Oberlin his conversation gave much pleasure and Lenz's graceful and childish face delighted him . . .

But only as long as daylight filled the valley could he endure it; towards evening a strange awe took possession of him, he felt like running after the sun; gradually, as objects became more shadowy, all appeared so dreamlike, so antagonistic to him; he was seized with fear, like children left to sleep in the dark, it seemed to him that he was blind. Now his terror grew, the nightmare of madness sat at his feet, the unalterable thought that all was only a dream opened to him; he clung to every object. Shapes passed swiftly before his eyes, he tried to hold them; they were shadows, the life was drained out of him, his limbs were quite paralysed. He spoke, he sang, he recited passages from Shakespeare, he clutched at everything that at another time would have made his blood flow more quickly, he tried everything, but cold, cold! He had to go out into the open air. What little light he could see strewn through the night, once his eyes had got used to the darkness, made him feel better; he hurled himself into the well, the stark effect of the water made him feel better; besides, he had secret hopes of an illness—and now he conducted his bathing less noisily.

But as he got used to his new way of life he grew calmer. He assisted Oberlin, sketched, read the Bible; old, discarded hopes reasserted themselves: the New Testament seemed so near to him here ... When Oberlin told him how an invisible hand had held him back on the bridge, how on the summit a radiance had dazzled his eyes, how he had heard a voice, how it had spoken to him in the night and how God had wholly entered his heart, so that like a child he would cast dice whenever he did not know what to do: this faith, this eternal Heaven on earth, this being in God—only now Holy Writ became quite clear to him. How close was nature to the people here, how close all the heavenly mysteries; yet neither violent nor majestic, but still familiar.

One morning he went out. It had snowed in the night; now the valley was filled with bright sunshine, though further away the landscape was half veiled in mist. He soon strayed from the path, up a gentle rise, no more trace of footsteps, a pine forest on one side; the sun was caught in crystals, the snow was light and flaky, here and there the track of wild animals softly

imprinted on the snow, leading into the mountains. Not
a movement in the air other than a soft breeze or the
faint rustle of a bird shaking snow from its tail. All so
still and far above, the trees with swaying white feathers
in the deep-blue air. Gradually the scene became familiar to him: the immense, uniform lines and planes,
whose aspect sometimes suggested to him that they
were addressing him with mighty voices, were shroud-
ed; a familiar feeling as of Christmas crept upon him:
sometimes he thought that his mother would step from
behind a tree to tell him that all these were her presents
to him; she would be tall as in those days. As he descended he saw that a rainbow of rays had gathered
around his shadow; he felt as though something had
touched his forehead: the created world was speaking
to him.

He came down. Oberlin was in the room, Lenz went
up to him gaily and told him that perhaps he would
deliver a sermon one day. 'Are you a theologian?'—
'Yes.'—'Good, next Sunday, then.'

Happy, Lenz went up to his room. He was thinking
about a text for a sermon and grew pensive, his nights
restful. Sunday morning came, the thaw had begun.
Clouds gliding past, blue in between. The church stood
nearby, up the mountain, on a projection, round about
it the churchyard. Lenz was standing up above when
the bell pealed and the church-goers, women and girls
in their grave black costumes, a white folded hand-
kerchief on each hymn-book and a spray of rosemary,
came up or down the narrow paths, between rocks
from various directions. Sometimes a glance of sunshine rested on the valley, the warm air stirred slowly,
the landscape swam in a sweet odour, distant ringing

of bells—it seemed as if everything were being merged in a single harmonious wave.

In the little churchyard the snow was gone, dark moss beneath black crosses; a belated rosebush leaned against the churchyard wall, belated flowers as well from under the moss; sometimes sunshine, then again darkness. The service began, the human voices met in a pure bright chord; an impression like that of looking into a clean, translucent mountain stream. The singing subsided, Lenz began to speak. He was diffident; under the spell of the music his inner convulsions had ceased, but now his whole agony stirred again and settled in his heart. A sweet sensation of infinite well-being came upon him. With those people he spoke simply, they suffered with him; and it was a comfort to be able to bring sleep to eyes that have wept themselves tired, peace to tormented hearts, to turn heavenwards this muted suffering of an existence tormented by material needs. He had become more confident as he concluded—but then the voices struck up again:

> 'Let the holy pain within me
> Release deep wells entirely;
> Let suffering be all my gain,
> Suffering be my service then.'

The urge within him, the music, the agony shattered him. The All seemed full of wounds; he felt deep, unspeakable pain bacause of it. Now for a different life: divine, twitching lips bent over him and attached themselves to his lips; he returned to his solitary room. He was alone, alone! Then the well gushed forth, streams broke from his eyes, he contorted himself, his limbs convulsed in a spasm, he felt as if he were about to dissolve, the voluptuous crisis seemed interminable. At last it grew dark inside him, he experienced a soft, profound compassion for himself, he wept for himself, his head sank down upon his chest, he went to sleep. A full moon hung in the sky; locks of hair fell on his cheeks —so he lay alone, and all was silent and still and cold, and the moon shone all night and hung above the mountains.

Next morning he came down and told Oberlin quite calmly how in the night his mother had appeared to him: dressed in white, she had stepped from the dark churchyard wall, a red and a white rose fastened to her breast; she had sunk down into a corner and slowly the roses had overgrown her—she must surely be dead; he was quite untroubled on that account.

In reply Oberlin described to him how he had been alone in a field at the time of his father's death and had heard a voice, so that he knew his father was dead; and when he went home he found that it was so. This led him to speak of other things, he told Lenz of the people in the mountains, about girls who could feel the presence of water and metal underground, about men who on many a mountain-top had been seized and had wrestled with a spirit; he told him also how once, by gazing into the deep void of a mountain pool, he had fallen into a kind of somnambulism. Lenz said that the spirits of the waters had come upon him, enabling him to feel something of his true nature. He went on: the simplest and purest individuals were most closely related to the elements; the more subtle a man's intellectual life and perceptions, the more blunted this sense of the elemental became; he did not consider it an exalted state of mind, because it was not independent enough, but he thought it must give one a sense of infinite bliss to be thus touched by the individual life of every form of creation, to have a soul that would communicate with stones, metals, water and plants, as in a dream to absorb into oneself every being in nature, as flowers absorb air according to the waxing and waning of the moon.

He expressed other ideas; how in all things there was an indescribable harmony, a tone, a blissfulness which in the higher forms required a greater number of organs to externalise themselves, to respond, to apprehend, but that consequently these were the more deeply susceptible; while in the lower forms all was more repressed, more limited, but consequently contained more repose. He pursued this further; Oberlin cut him short, it led him too far from his simple ways. Another time Oberlin showed him some small cakes of paint and explained to him in what manner each colour was related to human beings; he produced twelve apostles, each represented by one colour. Lenz understood, he spun out the thread even further, fell into fearful dreams, began, like Stilling,[1] to read the Apocalypse and studied the Bible assiduously.

At about this time Kaufmann[2] and his fiancée came to the Steintal. At first this visit displeased Lenz; he had, as it were, feathered a little nest for himself, and

[1] J. H. Jung-Stilling (1740-1817) was a Pietist; the first part of his long autobiographical novel was published by Goethe in 1777; five other volumes followed in the course of his life.
[2] Christoph Kaufmann (1753-1795) liver at Winterthur, Switzerland, where Lenz stayed with him for some months. He was the writer of abstruse tracts for the betterment of mankind and a protégé of Lavater's. He had made the acquaintance of Lenz at Weimar in 1776 and visited Lenz's relatives in Livonia during a tour of Europe in the following year. [*Transl.*]

this little bit of peace was so precious to him. And now
someone was coming to see him, somebody who reminded him of so much, with whom he must talk and
argue, somebody who knew his circumstances. Oberlin
knew nothing about his past; he had put him up, looked
after him, had regarded his coming as a piece of provi-
dence, for it was God who had sent him this unhappy
man; he loved Lenz with all his heart. Besides, Lenz's
presence was necessary to everyone there; he belonged
to them, as if he had long been with them, and no
one asked whence he had come and where he would
go.

During the meal Lenz recaptured his good mood;
they were talking about literature, he was on his own
ground. The idealistic movement was just beginning
at that time, Kaufmann was one of its supporters. Lenz
ardently opposed him. He said: 'Even the poets of
whom we say that they reproduce reality have no con-
ception of what reality is, but they're a good deal more
bearable than those who wish to transform reality.'
He said: 'I take it that God has made the world as it
should be and that we can hardly hope to scrawl or
daub anything better; our only aspiration should be
to re-create modestly in His manner. In all things I
demand—life, the possibility of existence, and that's all;
nor is it our business to ask whether it's beautiful,
whether it's ugly. The feeling that there's life in the
thing created is much more important than considerations of beauty and ugliness; it's the sole criterion in
matters of art. Besides, it's only rarely that we find this
quality; we find it in Shakespeare; it strikes us with
full impact in popular ballads and songs, only sometimes in Goethe; everything else should be thrown on

the fire. Those poor wretches aren't capable of drawing as much as a dog's kennel; ideal personages is what
they ask for, but all I've seen is a lot of wooden puppets.
This idealism is the most shameful contempt for human
nature. If only artists would try to submerge themselves in the life of the very humblest person and to
reproduce it with all its faint agitations, hints of experience, the subtle, hardly perceptible play of his features . . .' He himself had tried something of the kind
in his 'Private Tutor' and 'The Soldiers'.[3] 'These are the
most prosaic people in the world, but the emotional
vein is identical in almost every individual; all that
varies is the thickness of the shell which this vein must
penetrate. All one needs for these things is eyes and
ears in one's head. Yesterday, as I was walking along
the edge of the valley, I saw two girls sitting on a
stone; one of them was unfastening her hair, the other
was helping her. Her golden hair hung down; a grave,
pale face, and yet so young, and the black dress and the
other one so anxiously busying herself. The finest, most
intimate pictures of the German school can hardly give
us an idea of what this scene was like. Sometimes one
would like to be a Medusa's head, so as to be able to
transform such a group into stone and show it to
people. The girls got up, destroying this fine compo-
sition; yet as they were descending between the rocks
a new picture was made. The most beautiful pictures,
the richest harmonies group and dissolve. Only one
thing remains: an unending loveliness that moves from
one form to another, eternally undone, eternally changing. Of course one can't always hold on to it, put it

[3] *Der Hofmeister* (1774) and *Die Soldaten* (1775) are Lenz's
most successful plays. [*Transl.*]

into art galleries or bars of music and then fetch the old
and the young, let boys and old men chatter about it
and be filled with delight. One must love human nature
in order to penetrate into the peculiar character of any
individual; nobody, however insignificant, however
ugly, should be despised; only then can one understand
human kind as a whole. The most undistinguished face
can make a deeper impression than the mere perception
of abstract beauty, and one can allow one's characters
to emerge from one's own mind without copying in
any of the externals, without adding details in which
one feels no life, no muscles, no pulsations beating in
response to one's own.'

Kaufmann objected that in the real world he would
never find the prototype for an Apollo Belvedere or a
Madonna by Raphael. 'What does it matter?' Lenz replied; 'I must confess that they make me feel quite dead.
When I'm in a state of great mental activity they could,
perhaps, make me feel something, but then I should be
doing most of the work. Best of all I like that poet and
that visual artist who can reproduce nature for me with
the greatest degree of truthfulness, so that I can feel
his creation; everything else puts me off. I prefer the
Dutch painters to the Italian, because they're the only
ones I can grasp. I know only two pictures, and those
by Dutch or Flemish painters, that have given me an
impression comparable to that of the New Testament:
one of them, I don't know who painted it, is Christ
and the Disciples at Emmaus. When one reads how the
Disciples went forth, the whole of nature is in those
few words. It is a dim, twilit evening, a straight red
streak of red on the horizon, half dark in the street;
then a stranger approaches them, they speak, he breaks

bread; then they recognise Him, in a simply human manner, and the divinely suffering features speak to them distinctly, and they are frightened, for it is now dark and something incomprehensible confronts them; but there is nothing ghostly about their fear, it is as though someone we love and who is dead were to approach us at dusk in his old familiar way; that's what the picture is like, with its surface of monotonous brown, the dim, quiet evening. Then there's the other picture: a woman sitting in her room, a prayer-book in her hand. Everything is dressed in its Sunday best, sand has been strewn on the floor, all homely, clean and warm. The woman has been unable to go to church and she's conducting the service at home: the window is open, she sits inclined towards it, and it seems as if the sound of the village bells were drifting in through the windows, across the wide flat landscape, and the singing of the nearby congregation were reaching her faintly from the church, while the woman looks up the appropriate text.'

In this fashion they talked on; the others listened attentively, much of what Lenz said impressed them. He had become flushed as he spoke and, now smiling, now serious, shook his blond locks. He had quite forgotten himself.

After the meal Kaufmann took him aside. He had received letters from Lenz's father, who said his son must go back to assist him. Kaufmann told him that he was idling away his life here, wasting it recklessly, that he should set himself an aim—and more in this strain. Lenz turned on him: 'Leave here, leave? Go home? To go mad there? You know I can't bear to live anywhere but in these parts. If I weren't able to go up a mountain at times, to look at the scenery and then go down again to the house, through the garden, and then look in through the window—I'd go mad, I tell you, mad! Why don't you leave me alone? Just a little peace now that I'm beginning to feel almost well again. Go away? I don't understand you, those two words make a mess of the world. Everyone needs something; if he's able to rest, what more could he have? What's the use of continually climbing, struggling, eternally throwing away everything the moment gives you, continually suffering so as to enjoy some future state! To be thirsty while a bright spring flows across your path! Here life is bearable to me, and here I'll stay. Why, you ask, why? Simply because that's my will. What does my father want? What can he give me? Impossible! Leave me alone, all of you!' He was hot with anger; Kaufmann left. Lenz was upset.

On the following day Kaufmann wanted to go. He persuaded Oberlin to accompany him to Switzerland. The wish to become personally acquainted with Lavater,[4] whom he had long known by correspondence, decided him. He accepted; they had to spend one day on preparations. To Lenz this was a burden. In order to rid himself of his immeasurable torment he had clung anxiously to every person and thing around him. At

[4] J. G. Lavater (1741-1801), the Swiss theologian and moralist, famous in his lifetime for his physiognomical writings. His *Aphorisms on Man* were annotated by William Blake, who greatly admired his writings. Goethe's attitude to him was more critical. [*Transl.*]

certain moments it was clear to him that he was merely deceiving himself; he treated himself like a sick child. Some thoughts, some violent emotions he could not ward off without intense anxiety; then again he would suddenly be driven back to them with boundless urgency, he would tremble, his hair almost on end, until the enormous tension left him exhausted. He took refuge in a vision always hovering in front of his eyes, and in Oberlin whose words, whose face was unutterably soothing to him. So he awaited Oberlin's departure with fear.

The prospect of being left alone in the house at present was dreadful to him. The weather had turned mild, he decided to go with Oberlin into the mountains. On the other side, where the valleys became plains, they separated. He returned alone. He rambled over the mountains in various directions. Vast surfaces sloped down to the valleys, little wooded country, nothing but mighty lines and, further away, the wide, misty plain; in the air a powerful wind, not a trace of human life other than an occasional hovel—used by shepherds in summer, but now deserted—nestling against the slope. He grew calm, almost, perhaps, as if lost in a dream: everything seemed to melt, merged in a single line, like a rising and sinking wave between heaven and earth; he imagined he was lying on the shore of a boundless ocean that softly rose and fell. Sometimes he would sit down; then move on, but slowly, dreaming. He did not look for a way.

It was dark when he came to an inhabited cottage, on the slope leading down to the Steintal. The door was locked; he went to a window, drawn by a streak of light. A lamp illuminated little more than a single point: its light fell upon the pale face of a girl who, her eyes half-closed, slowly moving her lips, rested behind it. Further away in the dark an old woman sat singing out of a prayerbook, her voice harsh and throaty. After much knocking she opened the door; she was half-deaf. She served Lenz with some food and showed him a place where he could sleep, but never ceased chanting her song. The girl had not stirred. Some time later a man came in; he was tall and lean, traces of grey hair, with a restless, troubled face. He went up to the girl, she started and became restless. He took a dried herb from the wall and laid its leaves on her hand, so that she grew more quiet and hummed intelligible words in long-drawn, but piercing tones. The man told her how he had heard a voice in the mountains and had then seen sheet-lightning above the valleys; he had been seized bodily too and had wrestled with it like Jacob. He went down on his knees and prayed softly but fervently, while the sick woman sang in long-drawn, softly echoing tones. Then he settled down for the night.

Lenz dozed dreamily, but later heard the clock ticking in his sleep. The rushing of the wind made itself heard through the girl's low chanting and the old woman's voice, sometimes close, sometimes distant, and now bright, now clouded over, dreamlike the moon cast its changing light into the room. At one time the singing became louder, the girl spoke words both definite and distinct: she said that on the rock opposite there stood a church. Lenz looked up: she was sitting upright behind the table, her eyes wide open, and the moon shed its light upon her features, from which a ghostly glow seemed to radiate; at the same time the

old woman muttered hoarsely, and amidst this changing and sinking of the light, these sounds and voices,
Lenz at last fell into a deep sleep.

He awoke early. In the half-light of the room all
were asleep, even the girl had found some rest. She was
leaning back, her hands folded under her left cheek;
the ghostly glow had faded from her face, her expression now was one of indescribable suffering. He stepped up to the window and opened it, the cold morning
air struck his face. The house was situated at one end
of a low, narrow valley which opened towards the
east; red rays shot through the grey morning sky into
the half-light of the valley, deep in white mist, sparkled
against grey stones and pierced the windows of the
huts. The man awoke. His eyes met a lighted picture on
the wall and remained fixed upon it, without a flicker;
now he began to move his lips and prayed softly,
then loudly, then more loudly still. Meanwhile some
people entered the hut and, without so much as a word,
fell upon their knees. The girl was suffering from convulsions, the old woman was rattling out her song, and
chatting with the neighbours. The people told Lenz
that the man had come to this district a long time ago,
no one knew where from, he was reputed to be a saint,
he could see water underground and exorcise evil spirits,
and people went on pilgrimages to see him. At the same
time Lenz discovered that he had strayed further from
the Steintal; he left together with a party of wood-
cutters who were going towards those parts. He was
glad of the company; he now felt uneasy in the presence of that powerful man, who sometimes seemed
to him to be talking in horrible tones. Also he was
afraid of himself when in solitude.

He came home. But the night now past had left a deep impression. The world had been bright, and now he felt in himself a stirring and teeming towards an abyss into which a relentless power was dragging him. Now he was burrowing within himself. He ate little; many nights half spent in prayer and feverish dreams. A violent surging, and then beaten back exhausted; he lay bathed in the hottest tears and then suddenly acquired a strange strength, rose cold and indifferent; his tears seemed like ice to him then, he could not help laughing. The higher he raised himself by his efforts, the deeper down he was hurled again. Once more everything converged into one stream. Recollections of his old state of mind convulsed him and threw searchlights into the wild chaos of his mind.

In the daytime he usually sat in the room downstairs. Madame Oberlin went in and out of the room; he sketched, painted, read, clutched at every diversion, always hurriedly changing from one to another. But he felt particularly drawn to Madame Oberlin's company, when she was sitting there, the black hymn-book in front of her, next to a plant that had been reared inside the room, the youngest child between her knees; also he gave much attention to the child. Once he was sitting like this when he grew anxious, jumped up and began to walk about. The door ajar—then he heard the maid sing, unintelligibly at first, later he heard these words:

> 'In this world I have no joy at all
> But my sweetheart, and he's away.'

This struck home, the words and the intonation almost destroyed him. Madame Oberlin looked at him. He took heart, could no longer endure to be silent, he had to speak about it: 'Dearest Madame Oberlin, couldn't you tell me what's become of the lady[5] whose fate lies so heavy on my heart?'—'But Mr. Lenz, I don't know anything about it.'

Then he was silent once more and began to pace the room, briskly from one end to the other and back again; but soon he paused to say: 'Look here, I'll leave; O God, you're the only people with whom I could bear to live, and yet—and yet I must go, to *her*— but I can't, I mustn't.' He was greatly excited and left the house.

Towards evening Lenz returned, the room was in twilight, he sat down beside Madame Oberlin. 'You see,' he resumed, 'when she used to walk through the room, singing half to herself, and every step she took was a kind of music, there was so much happiness in her, and that overflowed into me, and I was always at peace when I looked at her or when she leaned her head against me, and—she was wholly a child; it seemed as if the world were too wide for her, she was so retiring, she would look for the narrowest place in the whole house, and there she'd sit as though all her happiness were concentrated into one little point, and then I thought so too; then I could have played like a child. Now I feel so hemmed in! so restricted! You see, some-times I feel my arms colliding with the sky; oh, I'm

[5] In 1772, at Sesenheim near Strasbourg, Lenz made himself ridiculous by courting Friederike Brion, for no other reason, it was said, than that Goethe had done so before him. One of Lenz's finest poems, *Die Liebe auf dem Lande*, deals with this episode; it should have served to vindicate his sincerity. [*Transl.*]

suffocating. And often at those moments I think I'm suffering physical pain, there, in the left side, in my arm with which I used to hold her. And yet I can no longer picture her, the image runs away from me, and that torments me; only at times everything becomes clear and bright and I feel quite well again.' Later he often returned to this subject when speaking to Madame Oberlin, but always incoherently; she could not reply at great length, but consoled him a little.

Meanwhile his religious torments continued. The emptier, the colder, the more dead he felt inwardly, the more he was urged to kindle some kind of heat within; he remembered the times when everything seethed within him, when the ardour of all his emotions made him breathless. And now so dead! He despaired of himself; then he went down on his knees, he wrung his hands, he stirred up everything that was in him—but all was dead, quite dead! Then he implored God to give him a sign, to work a miracle through him; then he tormented himself, fasted, lay on the floor in a dream.

On the 3rd of February he heard that a child had died at Fouday; Friederike was her name. He took this up like a fixed idea. He withdrew to his room and fasted for one day. On the 4th he suddenly entered Madame Oberlin's room; he had smeared his face with ashes and demanded an old sack. She was startled but gave him what he wanted. He wrapped the sack around himself like a penitent and set out for Fouday. The people in the village were already used to him; many a strange tale about him had circulated there. He entered the house where the dead child lay. The people were pursuing their business indifferently; he was shown to a room, the child was lying on straw placed on a wooden table, dressed in her shift.

Lenz shuddered when he touched her cold limbs and saw the half-open, glassy eyes. The child seemed so forsaken, and he himself so feeble and lonely. He threw himself down upon the dead body. Death frightened him, a violent agony overcame him; these features, this still face would have to decay—he went down on his knees, he prayed with all the anguish of despair that God might work a miracle through him and recall the child to life, weak and unhappy though he was: then he withdrew into himself and concentrated all his will-power upon one point. For a long time he sat there motionless. Then he rose and clasped the child's hands in his, and said loudly and earnestly: 'Arise and walk!' But soberly the walls echoed his voice, as though to mock him, and the corpse remained cold. Half mad, he collapsed on the floor; then terror seized him, he rushed out, and away into the mountains.

Clouds were passing swiftly across the moon; now all was in darkness, now the nebulous, vanishing landscape was revealed in the moonlight. He ran up and down. In his breast Hell was rehearsing a song of triumph. The wind sounded like the singing of Titans. He felt capable of clenching an enormous fist, thrusting it up into Heaven, seizing God and dragging Him through His clouds; capable of masticating the world with his teeth and spitting it into the face of the Creator; he swore, he blasphemed. Thus he arrived at the highest point of the mountains, and the uncertain light stretched down towards the white masses of stone, and the heavens were a stupid blue eye, and the moon, quite ludicrous, idiotic, stood in the midst. Lenz had to laugh loudly, and as he laughed atheism took root in him and possessed him utterly, steadily, calmly, relentlessly. He no longer knew what it was that had moved him so much before, he felt cold; he thought he would like to go to bed now, and went his way through the uncanny darkness, cold and unshakable—all was empty and hollow to him, he was compelled to run home, and went to bed.

On the following day he felt intense horror when he remembered his condition on the previous night. Now he stood on the brink of the abyss, where a mad desire urged him to look into its depths again and again and to repeat this torment. Then his fear increased, for what confronted him was nothing less than the sin against the Holy Ghost.

Some days later Oberlin returned from Switzerland much sooner than expected. Lenz was upset by this. But he became more cheerful when Oberlin told him about his friends in Alsace. Oberlin walked about the room, unpacked his things, put them away. He came to talk about Pfeffel,[6] praising the happiness of a country parson's life. Also he proceeded to advise Lenz to comply with his father's wishes, to take up his profession again, to return home. He told him: 'Honour thy father and thy mother,' and more in this strain. The conversation violently disquieted Lenz; he sighed deeply, tears welled from his eyes, he spoke abruptly: 'Yes, I know, but I can't bear it; do you want to drive me away? In

[6] G. C. Pfeffel (1736-1809), the author of poems and fables popular at one time, lived at Colmar. [*Transl.*]

you alone is the way to God. But it's all over with me!
I've fallen away, I'm damned for eternity, I'm the Wandering Jew.' Oberlin told him that this was precisely
what Jesus had died for, that he should turn to
Him with fervour and would then partake of His
mercy.

Lenz raised his head, wrung his hands and said: 'Ah!
Divine consolation!' Then, suddenly gracious, he asked
what had become of the lady. Oberlin replied that he
knew nothing whatever about her, but that he would
help him in all things; but Lenz must inform him of
the place, circumstances and of her identity. Lenz
answered incoherently: 'Oh, she's dead! Is she still
alive? You angel! She loved me, I loved her, she was
worthy of it—you angel! This damnable jealousy, I
sacrificed her—she loved another man also—I loved her,
she was worthy of it—O dear mother, she also loved
me. I'm a murderer!' Oberlin replied that perhaps all
these persons were still alive, contentedly perhaps; whatever their condition now, once Lenz had been wholly
converted in his heart, God could and would do so
much for them in answer to his prayers and tears that
the service he would have done them would perhaps
outweigh the harm he had already done. This gradually calmed Lenz, who went back to his painting.

In the afternoon he returned to Oberlin. On his left
shoulder he had placed a piece of fur and in his hand
he carried a bunch of birch rods, which he had been
asked to deliver to Oberlin together with a letter. He
gave the rods to Oberlin and asked him to beat him
with them. Oberlin took them from him, kissed him
several times on the mouth, and said: 'These are the
only strokes I can give you.' He asked him to calm

himself and to make his peace with God by himself, as any number of scourgings could not remove a single sin; Jesus had made that His business and it was to Him that Lenz should turn. Lenz went away.

During supper he was, as usual, somewhat pensive. Yet he spoke of one thing and another, but with anxious haste. At about midnight Oberlin was awakened by a noise. Lenz was running through the courtyard, calling out the name 'Friederikt' in a hollow, metallic voice, though in confusion and despair; he flung himself into the well, splashed about in it, out again and up to his room, down again to the well, and continued in this way several times. At last he grew quiet. The maids, who lived in the nursery immediately below his room, said they had often, but particularly during this same night, heard a moaning sound which they could compare only with the sound of a reed pipe. Perhaps it was Lenz whining in a hollow, terrible despairing voice.

Next morning Lenz did not appear at the usual time. At last Oberlin went up to his room; Lenz was lying in bed, rigid and motionless. Oberlin had to address him several times before he received an answer; at last Lenz said: 'Yes, vicar, you see it's boredom, boredom! Oh it's very boring! Really. I no longer know what to say. I've already drawn all sorts of figures on the wall.' Oberlin told him to direct his thoughts towards God, whereupon Lenz laughed and said: 'Yes, if I were as fortunate as you are, fortunate enough to find such a pleasant pastime, yes, in that case I imagine you could fill in the time quite pleasantly. All out of idleness: for most of us pray out of boredom, others fall in love out of boredom, some are virtuous and some are evil; only

I am nothing, nothing, and I don't even feel like doing
away with myself; it really is too boring!

> O God, in the wave of thy light,
> At thy noontide's glistening height,
> My long-waking eyes have grown sore.
> Shall the healing light come no more?'

Oberlin looked at him with displeasure and prepared to
go. Lenz flitted after him, fixing him with a ghastly
look: 'You see, now I have an idea after all, if I could
only distinguish whether I'm dreaming or awake; you
see, it's very important, we must look into it.' Then he
flitted back into bed.

In the afternoon Oberlin wished to pay a visit in the
neighbourhood. His wife had already left. He was about
to leave when someone knocked on the door, and Lenz
came in, his body bent forward, his head hanging down;
his whole face and part of his clothing covered with
ashes, his left hand supporting his right arm. He asked
Oberlin to pull his arm, since he had twisted it in the
act of throwing himself out of the window; but since
nobody had seen him do it he did not want anyone else
to know. Oberlin was violently shocked, but said nothing; he did what Lenz had asked him to do. Immediately
afterwards he wrote to the schoolmaster at Bellefosse,
asking him to come down, and giving him instructions;
then he rode away.

The man arrived. Lenz had often seen him before
and had become attached to him. The schoolmaster
pretended he had come to discuss certain matters with
Oberlin and would then leave. Lenz asked him to stay,
and so they remained together. Lenz suggested a walk
to Fouday. He visited the grave of the child whom he

had once tried to raise from the dead, knelt down several times, kissed the earth on the grave, seemed to be praying, but confusedly plucked up some of the flowers that grew on the grave, to keep as a souvenir, returned to Waldbach, turned back again, and Sebastian with him. Sometimes he walked slowly and complained of a great weakness in his limbs, then again with desperate haste; the landscape frightened him, it was so narrow that he was afraid of colliding with every object he could see. An indescribable feeling of discomfort came upon him, his companion began to be a burden to him; also, perhaps, he guessed his intentions, and now tried to get rid of him. Sebastian seemed to give in to him, but found secret means of informing his brother of the danger, and now Lenz had two keepers instead of one. He continued to drag them along with him; at last he returned to Waldbach, and as they approached the village, turned about quick as lightning and bounded away like a stag, in the direction of Fouday. While they were looking for him at Fouday, two shopkeepers approached them and told them that a stranger who confessed that he was a murderer had been arrested in one of the houses and had been bound, but that surely he could not be a murderer. They ran to the house and found it so. A young man, intimidated by Lenz's awkward gestures, had bound him. They released him and brought him safely to Waldbach, where they found Oberlin and his wife, who had returned in the meantime. Lenz looked confused. But when he found that his reception was kind and affectionate, his courage revived; his face changed favourably, he thanked his two escorts politely, even tenderly, and the evening passed quietly. Oberlin persistently implored him not to

take any more baths, to remain in his bed and to rest
during the night, and, if he could not sleep, to converse
with God. He promised, and did so the following night.
The maids heard him pray almost all night long.

The following morning he went up to Oberlin's room
in a cheerful mood. When they had discussed various
matters, he said with extreme gentleness: 'Dearest vicar,
the lady of whom I was telling you has died, yes died—
the angel!'—'How do you know that?'—'Hieroglyphics, hieroglyphics!' and then he looked heavenwards and said again: 'Yes, died—hieroglyphics!' Then
not another word could be got out of him. He sat down
to write some letters and gave them to Oberlin, asking
him to add a few lines to them.

Meanwhile his condition had become increasingly
hopeless. All the peacefulness he had drawn from Oberlin's companionship and the valley's stillness was gone;
the world which he had wished to put to some use had
suffered an immense rift; he felt no hatred, no love, no
hope—a terrible emptiness, and yet a torturing restlessness, an impatient impulse to fill this void. He possessed nothing. What he did he did consciously and yet
under the compulsion of an inner urge. When he was
alone he felt so horribly lonely that he constantly talked,
called out to himself in a loud voice, and then again
he was startled and it seemed as though a stranger's voice
had spoken to him. In conversation he frequently stut-
tered, an indescribable fear possessed him, he had lost
the conclusion of his sentence; then he thought he must
hold onto the word he had last spoken, say it again
and again, and it was only with greatest exertion of his

will that he suppressed these impulses. The good people were deeply grieved when sometimes, in his quieter moments, he sat with them and spoke without difficulty, and then suddenly began to stammer and an unspeakable fear was expressed in his features, when convulsively he seized the person nearest to him by the arm, and only gradually recovered himself. When he was by himself or reading a book, it was even worse; all his mental activity was often held up by a single word. If he thought about a stranger or if he pictured that person vividly to himself, then it was as if he himself became that person; he became utterly confused, and at the same time he felt an unending urge to do violence in his mind to every thing and person; nature, men and women, only Oberlin excepted—all was dreamlike, cold. He amused himself by mentally turning the houses upside down, dressing and undressing people, by thinking out the most extravagant pranks. Sometimes he felt an irresistible urge to carry out whatever project he happened to be hatching in his head, and then he made the most horrible faces. Once he was sitting next to Oberlin, the cat was lying opposite him on a chair. Suddenly his eyes became fixed, he kept them riveted upon the animal; then slowly he slipped off his chair, likewise the cat; it seemed to be spellbound by his gaze, grew immensely frightened, arched and bristled its back in terror, Lenz making catlike sounds, his face ghastly, distorted; as though in desperation they hurled themselves at each other, till at last Madame Oberlin rose to separate them. Then again he was deeply ashamed of himself. His nocturnal torments increased terribly. It was only with the greatest difficulty that he could go to sleep at all after first trying to fill the terrible void. Then between sleep and waking he fell into a dreadful state; he collided with some gruesome thing, it was horrible, madness clutched at him; he started up, bathed in sweat, uttered the most piercing shrieks, and only gradually came to himself again. Then he had to begin with the simplest objects in order to come to his senses. Really it was not he who did so, but a powerful instinct of self-preservation; he seemed to be split in two, with one part of him trying to save the other and calling out to itself; gripped by the most violent fear, he would recite poems again and again or tell himself stories until he recovered himself.

Even in the daytime he had these attacks, and then they were still more terrible; previously daylight had saved him from them. Then it seemed to him that he alone existed, that the world was only a fragment of his imagination, that there was nothing but he himself, and he the eternally damned, Satan, left to himself and to his painful imaginings. He tore through his past life with blinding speed, and then said: 'Consequential, consequential'; if somebody spoke, he said: 'Inconsequential, inconsequential';—it was the cleft of irremediable madness, a madness throughout eternity.

The urge for self-preservation would surprise him, he would fling himself into Oberlin's arms, cling to them as though he wanted to take refuge inside him. Oberlin was the only person who was alive to him and through whom life was still revealed to him. Then gradually Oberlin's voice would recall him to his senses; he would kneel down before him, his hands resting in Oberlin's hands, his face covered with cold sweat but resting on Oberlin's lap, his whole body trembling and heaving. Oberlin's pity for him was endless, the family were on their knees, praying for Lenz in his misery, the maids ran away and took him for one possessed. And when he grew calmer his sorrow was like a child's; he sobbed, he felt deep, deep compassion for himself; and these were his happiest moments. Oberlin spoke to him about God. Lenz quietly freed himself and looked at him with an expression of infinite suffering, finally saying: 'But if I were almighty, you see, if I were that, I should not tolerate all this suffering, I should save, save; for all I want is peace, peace so that I can sleep a little.' Oberlin told him this was blasphemy. Lenz shook his head disconsolately.

His half-hearted attempts at suicide, which occurred regularly during this period, were not wholly serious. It was not so much the desire for death—since for him there was neither peace nor hope in death—as an attempt to recall himself to consciousness through physical pain, in moments of terrible fear or of a blank calm that bordered on non-existence. Those times at which his mind seemed to be riding on some weird and eccentric idea were still his best. Then at least he was almost at peace, and his wild eyes were not as terrifying as in those moments of fear seeking for salvation, as in his unending torment of unrest. Often he beat his head against the wall or in some other way caused himself violent physical pain.

On the morning of the 8th he remained in bed. Oberlin went to see him; he lay there almost naked and was greatly excited. Oberlin wished to cover him, but Lenz complained bitterly, saying that all was so heavy, so very heavy! that he did not think he could walk at all, that never before had he felt the immense weight of the air. Oberlin spoke to him encouragingly, but Lenz remained in the same position and would not stir during the greater part of the day, nor would he take any food.

Towards evening Oberlin was called away to see a sick person at Bellefosse. The weather was mild and the moon was out. On his way home he met Lenz, who seemed quite reasonable and spoke to Oberlin in a calm and friendly manner. Oberlin asked him not to go too far away; he promised. As he was moving off, he suddenly turned about, came quite close to Oberlin and said quickly: 'You see, vicar, if only I didn't have to listen to that any more, I'd be cured.'—'Listen to what, my dear fellow?'—'Can't you hear it then? Can't you hear the terrible voice that is crying out the whole length of the horizon and which is usually known as silence? Ever since I came to the quiet valley I've heard it incessantly, it won't let me sleep; yes, vicar, if only I could sleep again some day!'—Then, shaking his head, he moved on.

Oberlin returned to Waldbach, intending to send somebody back for Lenz, when he heard him walk up to his room. A moment later something burst in the courtyard with such a mighty noise that Oberlin thought it could not possibly be caused by the fall of a human body. The nursemaid came up to him, deathly pale and trembling all over . . .[7]

With cold resignation he sat in the carriage as they drove west along the valley. He did not care where

[7] The gap in Büchner's story alluded to in the introduction occurs here. The reason why the nursemaid was 'deathly pale

they were taking him. Several times, when the carriage
was endangered by the roads, he remained sitting there,
perfectly calm; he did not care at all. In this state of
mind he passed over the mountains. Towards evening
they reached the Rhine valley. They gradually left the
mountains behind; now like a crystal wave the mountains rose against the red sky, a deep blue crystal wave
on whose warm flood the red rays of evening played;
a shimmering, bluish web covered the plain at the foot
of the mountain range. It grew darker as they approached Strasbourg; a high, full moon, all the more
distant landmarks in darkness, only the mountain nearest to them still in sharp relief; the earth was like a
golden cup over which the gold waves of the moon ran
foaming. Lenz stared at it all, not an idea, not an emotion inside him; only a blunted fear that grew more
intense as the landmarks lost themselves more and more
in the darkness. They had to turn in for the night.
Then once again he made several attempts to lay hands
on himself, but he was too well guarded.

On the following morning, in dull, rainy weather,
he arrived in Strasbourg. He seemed quite reasonable,
and talked to all sorts of people. He did everything

and trembling all over' is that Lenz had just made another
attempt at suicide by throwing himself out of the window. At
this point Oberlin decided that Lenz could not remain in his
house; he sent for two men to act as guards until he could be
removed to Strasbourg, but before their arrival Lenz attempted
to stab himself with a pair of scissors. In the course of the night
he proved too strong for two men; a third was called in, but
Lenz told them that even three would never cope with him.
Oberlin managed to calm him by kindness and by consenting
to pray for his soul. Later that day, Lenz agreed to his removal
to Strasbourg and left, as Büchner relates, but with the same
three men to guard him. [*Transl.*]

just as the others did; but there was a terrible emptiness inside him, he no longer felt any fear, any desire,
his existence was a burden to him, a burden he must
bear.

So he lived on . . .

A VILLAGE ROMEO AND JULIET
GOTTFRIED KELLER

Translated by Ronald Taylor

INTRODUCTION

GOTTFRIED KELLER, one of the greatest narrative writers of German literature, was born in Zürich in 1819. His family was poor and his education rudimentary, and after leaving school at fifteen he took up the study of painting, first in Zürich, then in Munich. But his faith in his artistic calling was not matched by his talent, and after two years in Munich he returned to his native town.

Turning his mind to writing instead of painting, he succeeded in having a group of poems published in a literary magazine, and on the basis of the promise which these poems revealed, he received a grant from the government of his canton to study at a university abroad. With this he went to Heidelberg, where he came under the strong influence of the materialist philosopher Feuerbach. After two years he left for Berlin, where he stayed from 1850 to 1855, publishing a further volume of poems and completing his first and most important novel, the autobiographical romance *Der grüne Heinrich*. Immediately after this he began to work at great speed on the succession of short stories by which he is best known today: those collected into two volumes under the title *Die Leute von Seldwyla*.

In 1855 Keller returned to Switzerland, and in 1861 was offered a position in the cantonal administration of Zürich. This post he held for fifteen years, during which time he published his *Sieben Legenden* and the cycle of historical stories *Zürcher Novellen*. He died in Zürich in 1890, four days before his seventy-first birthday.

It is in his shorter narrative works that Keller is seen at his strongest and most gripping. His subject-matter is often of slender proportions, and its setting provincial, but the pitiless penetration of his gaze and the blunt insistence of his manner—he was no respecter of persons—create from it works of ruthless characterisation and rugged situational power. He is no polished stylist, like his contemporary and countryman Conrad Ferdinand Meyer; indeed, his descriptive writing is often repetitious and technically inept, and one must sometimes wonder that it does not seriously detract from the effectiveness of the finished product. Yet the forceful realism of that product remains unshakeable— a blend of his observed experience of the people about whom he wrote and his relentless pursuit of significant detail.

The genesis of *Romeo und Julia auf dem Dorfe* lies in a Zürich newspaper report of the suicide of two young lovers who have been driven to desperation by the antagonism between their two families. Keller read this report at the time and sought to provide from his imagination a series of circumstances that could have led to a family feud; and the circumstances that he created were made to bear the motivation both of the degradation of the rival families and the ultimate tragedy of the lovers.

But for all his eloquent presentation of their tragic love, Keller has concerns that go beyond the personal

fate of Sali and Vrenchen, for these two unhappy creatures are but the helpless victims of forces that issue
from the evil ways of others; and these others,
moreover, are Keller's fellow-citizens from the locality
of his symbolical town of Seldwyla. The malice and
intolerance of the fathers; the thinly-veiled hostility
of most of the onlookers; jealousy that so complete
and pure a love should be vouchsafed to, of all people,
the children of such despicable families; and the Black
Fiddler's devilish attempts to seduce the lovers into exchanging a life of lighthearted abandon in his kingdom
of immoral freedom for their doomed existence among
the cruelties of a so-called moral society: these are the
malevolent realities that condition the lives of Vrenchen and Sali. And there is no simple, benevolent deity
who can be called upon to officiate at the restoration
of a simple, benevolent, optimistic faith. It is characteristic of Keller's forthrightness that this situation is
left—and resolved—in the realistic, uncompromising
terms that express his own view of life and human fate.

R.T.

PRINCIPAL DATES IN THE LIFE OF
GOTTFRIED KELLER

1819 Born in Zürich on July 19th.

1834 Expelled from school and took up the study of painting.

1840–42 Study of art in Munich.

1845 Publication of his first poems under the title *Lieder eines Autodidakten.*

1848–50 Study at Heidelberg on a scholarship from the cantonal government of Zürich.

1850–55 Residence in Berlin.

1851 *Neuere Gedichte.*

1854–55 Publication of *Der grüne Heinrich* (a revised edition was published in 1880).

1856 First volume of *Die Leute von Seldwyla* (five stories, including *Romeo und Julia auf dem Dorfe, Die drei gerechten Kammacher* and *Spiegel das Kätzchen*).

1861–76 *Staatssekretär* of the canton of Zürich.

1872 *Sieben Legenden.*

1874 Second volume of *Die Leute von Seldwyla* (including *Kleider machen Leute*).

1878 *Zürcher Novellen* (historical stories).

1883 *Gesammelte Gedichte.*

1890 Died in Zürich on July 15th.

A VILLAGE ROMEO AND JULIET

WERE this tale not based on actual occurrence, it would be mere idle repetition on my part to relate it. Yet how deeply rooted in human life is each and every one of the stories on which the great works of the past are built. For such stories, though few in number, constantly reappear in new guises and force themselves upon our attention.

From the banks of the beautiful river that flows past Seldwyla, about half-an-hour's walk from the town, there rises a gentle ridge which, lush and fertile, merges into the rolling plain beyond. At the foot of the slope lies a village with a number of large farmsteads, and years ago three long fields used to stretch out side by side above it, like three giant ribbons.

One sunny September morning two farmers were busy ploughing on the two outer fields; the field in the centre appeared to have lain fallow for many years, for it was full of stones and tall weeds, and a myriad creatures winged their untroubled way across its rustling grasses. The farmers, each tramping behind his plough, were tall, gaunt men of about forty who conveyed at first glance the air of prosperous and industrious husbandmen. They were wearing coarse knickerbockers whose every pleat had its permanent place, as though it were chiselled out of stone. When-

ever they met some obstacle, they gripped the plough
more tightly, and the sleeves of their rough shirts rip-
pled under the strain; alert yet relaxed, their clean-
shaven faces puckered slightly against the bright sunshine, they gauged their furrows, occasionally looking round when some distant sound disturbed the tranquillity of the scene.

Deliberately and with a certain natural grace they
each moved forwards step by step. Neither of them
spoke, save to give an order to the boy who was leading the fine horses. From a distance they looked identical representatives of the countryside at its most
characteristic; to a closer view they appeared distinguish-
able only in that one had the flap of his white cap
at the front, the other at the back. But this changed
when they ploughed in the opposite direction, for as
they met and passed at the top of the ridge, the strong
east wind blew the cap of the one back over his head,
while that of the other, who had the wind behind him,
was blown forwards over his face. And at each turn
there was a moment when the two caps stood erect,
quivering in the wind like two white tongues of
flame.

Thus the two men worked peacefully on, affording
a pleasant prospect in the stillness of the golden autumn
landscape as they passed each other silently at the top of
the slope, drew further and further apart again and
finally vanished behind the ridge like two setting stars,
only to appear again a short while later. If they found
a stone in one of the furrows, they tossed it on to the
field in the middle, but this happened only rarely, since
almost all the stones that had ever lain there were now
piled up on this centre field.

The long morning had run part of its course when a neat little cart was seen approaching the gentle slope from the village. It was a tiny green perambulator in which the children of the two farmers, a boy and a frail, delicate girl, were carrying up the morning meal. For each man there was a tasty sandwich wrapped in a serviette, a jug of wine and a glass, together with a few extra trifles which the wives had sent along for their hardworking husbands. Besides this, the perambulator contained a motley assortment of odd-shaped apples and pears which the children had found lying on the ground and started to eat; and finally there was a one-legged doll with a dirty face and no clothes, which was sitting between the sandwiches like a lady of rank riding elegantly in her carriage.

After stopping many times on the way, the little conveyance at last bumped its way to the top of the slope and stopped in the shade of a linden bush at the edge of the field, where it became possible to observe the two 'coachmen' more closely. The boy was seven, the girl five, both sound in wind and limb, and the only striking feature about them was that they both had very attractive eyes, while the girl's dark complexion and curly black hair gave her an intense, passionate look.

The farmers had now reached the top again. Stopping their ploughs in the half-completed furrow and leaving their horses some fodder, they walked across to where their meal was waiting and bade each other good morning, for they had not yet exchanged a word that day. As they sat there contentedly, good-humouredly sharing their food with the children, who did not leave until the two men had finished eating and drinking, they

gazed out over the countryside and contemplated the
smoke-shrouded village nestling in the hills: for when
the people of Seldwyla cooked their tasty lunch, a
silver haze hovered above the roofs of their houses,
shining for miles around and floating serenely up into
the mountains.

'Those rascals in Seldwyla are getting another good
meal ready,' said Manz, one of the farmers. Marti, the
other, rejoined:

'Someone came to see me yesterday about this field.'

"Someone from the Bezirksrat?'[1] asked Manz. 'He
came to my house too.'

'Well, well. And I suppose he suggested that you
should use the land and pay the council rent for it.'

'Yes, until it is decided who owns it and what is to
be done with it. But I refused to clear the place up for
somebody else, and told them to sell the field and keep
the money until the owner is found—which will probably never happen, because the authorities in Seldwyla
take ages over everything, and in any case it is a
difficult matter to settle. The rogues are all too eager
to feather their own nests by renting the field. And it
would be the same if they sold it—although you and I
would take care not to drive the price too high! At
least we would know then where we stood and who
the land belonged to.'

'That is just what I think, and I told the fellow so.'

They were silent for a while, then Manz said:

'Still, it is a pity to see good ground left in this state.
For almost twenty years nobody has troubled about it.
There is no one in the village with any claim to it, nor

---

[1] A public body roughly corresponding to a local district
council. [*Transl.*]

does anyone know what has become of the children of that wastrel, the Trumpeter.'

'Hm, a fine thing that would be!' retorted Marti. 'Whenever I look at the Black Fiddler, who spends half his time with the gypsies and the other half playing for village dances, I could almost swear that he is one of the Trumpeter's grandchildren. Of course, he does not know that he owns the field, but what would he do with it? Get drunk on the proceeds for a month and then go on living as before! In any case, since no one can be sure, who is going to raise the subject?'

'And it might have unpleasant consequences,' rejoined Manz. 'We've already got enough on hand to prevent this wretched Fiddler from settling in our community. People are constantly trying to foist him on to us. If his parents went off to join the gypsies, let him stay there and scrape his fiddle for them. How in Heaven's name are we expected to know that he is the Trumpeter's grandson? Even if his swarthy face does remind me of the Trumpeter, I tell myself that no man is infallible, and the smallest scrap of paper, a mere fragment of a birth certificate, would satisfy my conscience better than a dozen wicked faces!'

'Quite right!' exclaimed Marti. 'He says it is not his fault that he was not baptized, but does he expect us to carry our font out into the woods? We shall never do such a thing! Our font belongs in our church. If anything is to be carried around, let it be the bier that hangs outside on the church wall. The village is overcrowded already, and soon we shall need two more schoolteachers.'

With this the farmers finished their meal and their conversation, and got up to resume their morning's work. The two children, who were going to return home with their fathers, pushed the cart into the shade of the little linden trees and embarked on an expedition into the strange waste land with its creepers, its bushes and its piles of stones. After wandering hand in hand across the green wilderness for a while, joyfully swinging their arms over the tall thistle bushes, they sat down in the shade of one of these bushes, and the girl began to dress her doll with long leaves from the plants growing at the side of the path: she gave it a pretty green dress with jagged edges, and a bonnet made from a lone red poppy that was still in bloom, tied on with a blade of grass. The little creature looked like a sorceress, and even more so when it was given a necklace and girdle of little red berries.

Setting it on top of the bush, they both regarded it for a while. Then the boy, tired of looking at it, knocked it down with a stone and disarranged its clothes. The girl quickly took them off in order to dress it again, but as the doll lay there, naked except for the red bonnet, the impetuous boy snatched it away from her and hurled it high into the air. With tears in her eyes she tried to catch it, but he caught it first, threw it up again and teased her as she vainly tried to get her hands on it.

As a result of this treatment, however, the doll's only leg became damaged at the knee, where grains of bran began to trickle through a little hole. As soon as the tormentor noticed the hole, he stopped, looked at it open-mouthed and eagerly began to widen it with his nails, so as to see where the bran came from. The girl became suspicious at his silence, rushed over to him and saw with horror what he was doing.

'Look!' he cried, swinging the doll round in front of her, so that the bran flew out into her face. With a scream she tried to reach it, imploring him to give it to her, but he ran away, swinging the miserable toy round and round until its leg hung down limply like an empty bag. Finally he flung it to the ground, putting on an air of haughty disdain as she threw herself tearfully on top of it and wrapped it in her apron. As she uncovered it again and saw its leg hanging down from its body like a salamander's tail, she started to cry afresh.

But seeing her weep so bitterly, the mischievous boy began to feel sorry for what he had done. When she saw him standing there repentent and uneasy, she suddenly stopped and hit him several times with the doll, whereupon he cried out 'Ouch! Ouch!' and pretended to be hurt. So realistically did he do this, that she was appeased, and proceeded to help him dismember and destroy the doll. They bored hole after hole in it, letting the bran run out and carefully putting it in a heap on a flat stone, sifting it and looking at it closely.

The only part of the doll still intact was its head, which now claimed the children's particular attention. Removing it from its battered body, they peeped curiously into its interior. As they looked at the hollow cavity and at the bran, they were both seized by the same obvious thought, and raced each other to pour the bran into the head, which thereby came to have something in it for the first time. But the boy still seemed to regard this as useless knowledge, for suddenly he caught a large bluebottle, and while it buzzed inside his cupped hand, he told the girl to empty the bran out

of the doll's head. Then he put the bluebottle inside
and stuffed the head with grass. They held it to their
ears and then stood it solemnly on a stone, where, still
bedecked with the red poppy, and with the buzzing
sound coming from it, it looked like an oracle, to whose
parables and pronouncements the children listened in
complete silence as they sat there together.

But every prophet evokes ingratitude and fear. The
modicum of life in the pitiful little image aroused the
children's cruel instincts, and they resolved to bury it
alive. So they dug a hole and, without asking the insect's
opinion, put the head in it and solemnly erected a cairn
of stones at the head of the grave. But then they began
to shudder at the thought that they had buried a real
living creature, and they moved some distance away
from the eerie spot. The little girl was tired and lay
down on a soft, fragrant bank, chanting a few words
in monotonous sequence, while the boy crouched beside her, wondering whether he too should lie down,
so lazy and dreamy did he feel.

The sun shone down on her beautiful white teeth
and crimson lips as she lay there singing. Holding her
head in his hands and looking intently at her teeth, he
said:

'Guess how many teeth you have!'

Pretending to count them up in her mind, she cried
out impulsively:

'A hundred!'

'No, thirty-two!' he replied. 'I'll count them!'

And he began to do so, but because he could never
make them add up to thirty-two he kept starting over
again. She lay still for a long time, then, since he could
never finish his excited counting, she sat up and said:

'Now it's my turn to count yours!'

So he lay down on the grass with his mouth open, and she grasped his head and counted:

'One, two, seven, five, two, one . . .' for she had not yet learned to count. The boy corrected her and taught her to count properly, so that time after time she too had to start again from the beginning. Of all the games they had played that day, this seemed to give them the greatest delight. Tired out at last, however, the little girl sank down on to the body of her mentor, and the two children fell asleep in the bright midday sunshine.

Meanwhile their fathers had finished ploughing, leaving behind them the fresh brown fields. As one of the boys came to the end of the last furrow and was about to stop, the farmer shouted:

'What are you stopping for? Turn round again!'

'But we've finished,' protested the lad.

'Hold your tongue and do as you're told!' shouted the farmer.

So they turned round and carved a deep furrow in the middle field, sending the weeds and the stones flying up on both sides. The farmer did not stop to clear them away, apparently thinking there was plenty of time to do that later, but contented himself for the moment with getting the hardest part of the job done. On he ploughed up the gentle slope, and when he reached the top, where the breeze blew the tip of his cap backwards again, his neighbour passed him on the other side with his cap pointing forwards, also ploughing a wide furrow from the field in the middle and throwing up great clods of earth. Each saw clearly enough what the other was doing but pretended not to. Passing each other without a word, they went their separate ways like two constellations setting beneath the horizon.

Thus do the shuttles of destiny pass back and forth, and as the saying goes, 'What he weaves, no weaver knows'.[2]

Harvest followed harvest, the children grew taller and more handsome each year, and the unclaimed field grew narrower and narrower under the two neighbours' ploughs. Neither man uttered a word about it, neither man even seemed to see what wrong he was doing. Along the whole length of the field the stones were piled up on an ever-dwindling strip in the middle, like a mountain ridge, and the wild creepers that grew on it were soon so high that, although the children had grown so tall, they could not see each other from their own sides.

They no longer went out to the field together, for Sali, as the ten-year-old Salomon was called, now took his place at the side of the youths and men, while the vivacious, dark-skinned Vrenchen was made to stay in the company of her own sex lest she should be laughed at for being a tomboy. Nevertheless, when everybody else was busy on the field, they clambered up on to the stony ridge that separated them and played at pushing each other down. Their fathers' field met at no other point and since this was now the only contact that they had with each other, they seemed to celebrate the annual occasion all the more eagerly.

It had now been finally decided, however, that the

[2] A phrase taken from Heine. [*Transl.*]

field was to be sold and the money held in trust for the time being. The auction was held at the side of the field itself, but apart from Manz and Marti only a handful of idle bystanders were present, since nobody was interested in acquiring or cultivating this strange plot which separated the two neighbours. For although Manz and Marti were among the best farmers in the village, and had only acted as three-quarters of the rest would have done in the circumstances, people looked at them uneasily and had no desire to own the narrow strip which lay between their two fields. Most men are willing to commit certain common misdeeds if the temptation is put under their noses. But when one man has committed such a misdeed, the others are relieved that it was he who did it and not they, and that the temptation had not been theirs. They make the offender into a yardstick by which to measure their own sins, and treat him with modest deference as the one singled out by the gods to bear the common guilt; yet at the same time their mouths water at the thought of the pleasures that he has enjoyed.

Thus Manz and Marti were the only ones who bid seriously for the field. After a considerable struggle Manz finally succeeded in outbidding his neighbour, and the field was knocked down to him. The officials and the onlookers left the scene, and the two farmers, who both intended to finish some work on their fields, met as they moved away.

'I suppose,' said Marti, 'you will now put your fields together, the old one and the new, and divide them into two equal parts. At least, that is what I would do if I had bought the thing.'

'That's just what I'm going to do,' replied Marti. 'As

a single field it would be too big. But there's something
I wanted to say to you. I noticed the other day that
at the bottom of this field that now belongs to me, you
had driven your plough in from the side and cut off
quite a fair-sided triangular piece. You probably thought
that the whole field would soon become yours in any
case. But as it now belongs to me, you will realise that
I cannot have a crooked edge like that in it, so you
can hardly object if I straighten it again. We shan't
quarrel over that.'

'I see no cause for quarrel either,' replied Marti in
the same even tone. 'As far as I am concerned, you
have bought the field as it stands now. We all inspec-
ted it an hour ago, and since then it hasn't changed in
the slightest.'

'Fiddlesticks!' cried Manz. 'What's past is past! But
sometimes matters go too far, and when all is said and
done, a thing has to be properly settled. Right from
the beginning these two fields have been dead straight.
What strange quirk is it that makes you want to intro-
duce such an ugly shape? What sort of reputation
would we get if we left it crooked? The odd corner
has simply got to go!'

Marti laughed and retorted:

'What a remarkable concern you suddenly show that
people might laugh at you! Still, I suppose you can do
it if you want to, though the crooked line does not
worry me in the least. So if it annoys you, let's make
it straight, but not on my side—and I'll put that in
writing if you want it!'

'There's no point in joking,' said Manz. 'It is going
to be made straight, and on your side, too. So you can
put that in your pipe and smoke it!'

'We'll see about that,' snapped Marti, and the two men parted company without another glance, each glaring in front of him as though his whole attention were riveted on something in the distance.

The next day Manz sent out a farm-hand, a servant girl and his own son Sali to the field to pull up the weeds and the briers and put them on to heaps so that it would be easier to carry the stones away later. That Sali, who was barely eleven years old and had never been made to do any manual work before, should now be sent out with the others in spite of his mother's protestations, signified a change in his father's nature. He accompanied this decision with soft and soothing words, as though wishing to use his harshness towards his own flesh and blood as a means of quelling the sense of injustice which ruled his life and now began to run its slow, sinister course.

Cheerfully the little group pulled up the weeds and hacked away busily at the mass of strange plants and bushes which had grown up there over the years. It was the sort of unorganised work that required no particular care or skill but was looked on rather as enjoyment. All this foliage, dried out by the sun, was piled up and burnt with great jubilation; the smoke was blown far and wide, and the young folk leapt about like souls possessed.

This was the last celebration that the ill-starred field was to know. Young Vrenchen, Marti's daughter, also came out to help with the work. The unusualness of the occasion and the air of excitement that surrounded it were good enough reasons for her to join her young playmate again, and the two children were cheerful and happy as they danced round the fire. Other chil-

dren came as well, making a joyful party. But whenever
Sali became separated from Vrenchen, he tried to hunt
her out again, while she too, laughing with delight,
always managed to slip back to him, so that they both
felt that this wonderful day should never be allowed to
end.

Towards evening old Manz arrived to see how the
work had progressed, and although they had already
finished, he scolded them for their frivolity and broke
up the celebrations.

At the same time Marti appeared on his field. Catching sight of his daughter, he put his fingers in his mouth
and let out a shrill, imperious whistle. She hastened
across to his side, and without really knowing why,
he gave her a few sound cuffs on the head. The two
children burst into tears and made their way sadly
home, knowing as little why they were now so miserable as why they had been so happy a moment ago. In
their innocence they could not understand the reason
for this streak of cruelty that had recently appeared in
their fathers' characters, and it therefore did not arouse
any deeper emotions in them.

For the harder work of the next few days, when
Manz had the stones shovelled up and carted away,
the farm-hands were needed. It was an endless task:
all the stones in the world seemed to have collected
there. But instead of removing them from the field altogether, he had each cart-load emptied on to the disputed triangular area which Marti had carefully
ploughed. Drawing a straight line to mark the bound-
ary, he dumped on to this little piece of land all the
stones which they had both thrown over for as long
as they could remember. The result was a large pyra-

mid which he was convinced his adversary would do nothing to remove.

This was the last thing that Marti had bargained for; in fact, he had reckoned that the other man would go on ploughing as usual. He had therefore waited at home until he saw Manz go out, and only when the job was almost done did he hear about the fine monument that Marti had erected. Livid with rage, he rushed out, saw the hideous pile of stones, rushed back again and fetched the bailiff in order to register an immediate protest and have the land officially requisitioned. From this moment onwards the two men were locked in continuous legal battle, and did not rest until they had brought about their utter ruin and destruction.

Wise and reasonable as they normally were, Manz and Marti were now incapable of seeing beyond their own noses. The most petty legalistic thoughts filled their minds, and neither had the ability or the desire to understand how the other could behave in such a palpably unjust manner and wilfully appropriate this miserable bit of land to himself. In addition, Manz had a remarkable sense of symmetry, and was deeply offended by the stupid obstinacy with which Marti insisted on preserving the senseless and arbitrary crookedness of the field.

They each shared the conviction, however, that the other, in his impertinent and insolent way, must consider him a despicable fool, since one could only mete out such treatment to an unprincipled rogue, never to an upright citizen. Each thus felt his honour peculiarly offended and gave himself up passionately to the quarrel and to the resulting moral corruption. Their lives became like the tortured dream of two

condemned souls who fight with each other on a narrow plank which is drifting down a murky stream:
they beat the air, then, in the belief that they have laid
hands on their own misery, seize and finally destroy
each other.

Since their entire case was corrupt, they both fell a
ready prey to the worst kinds of trickster, who inflamed their perverted imaginations and filled their
minds with the most despicable thoughts. Most of these
enterprising gentry, for whom the whole affair was a
gift from the gods, belonged to the town of Seldwyla,
and in a short time the two enemies each had their
retinue of mediators, scandal-mongers and advisers
who knew a hundred ways of relieving a man of his
money.

The little triangle of land with its pile of stones, on
the top of which a forest of thistles and nettles had
already started to grow, had now become merely the
seed, the starting-point, of a disordered situation and
a meaningless life, in which these two fifty-year-old
men adopted attitudes and habits, hopes and principles,
quite different from those by which they had lived
hitherto. The more money they wasted, the more eagerly
they sought after it; and the less each had, the more
determined he grew to outdo his neighbour in getting rich. They were taken in by every fraud, and year
in, year out, they bet on all the lotteries in the
country, whose tickets circulated in Seldwyla in large
numbers.

But they never won a penny. Instead, they kept hearing of other people's success and of how they themselves
had almost won. Yet this passion continued to provide
a regular outlet for their money, and sometimes the

inhabitants of Seldwyla played a trick on them by having them share the same lottery ticket, so that they both set their hopes for ruining each other on one and the same number.

Half their time they spent in the town of Seldwyla, each establishing himself in some dingy cafe. Allowing their tempers to become inflamed, they were persuaded to part with their money in the most shameful ways and to give themselves over to a dissipated life of carousing. Yet at the same time they were sick at heart, for whereas they were really only carrying on the quarrel so as not to be taken for fools, they were now regarded by everyone as two of the biggest fools that had ever lived.

For the other half of the time they either stayed sullenly at home or went about their work, trying feverishly to make up for the time they had wasted and driving away all their good and trustworthy labourers in the process.

Things went rapidly from bad to worse. They were soon heavily in debt and clinging desperately to what was left to them, as vulnerable and as insecure as one-legged storks at the mercy of the wind. But however bad things became, the hatred between them grew ever greater for each regarded the other as the sole cause of his misfortune, his arch-enemy, the adversary whom the Devil had deliberately sent into the world to wreak his downfall. Even if they caught sight of each other from a distance, they would spit on the ground, and all contact between wives, children and servants was forbidden on pain of the severest punishment.

The two women reacted in different ways to the situation. Marti's wife, a good, upright woman, could

not endure it, and died of grief before her daughter
had reached the age of fourteen.

Manz's wife, on the other hand, adapted herself to
the change, and needed only to give free rein to certain inborn feminine frailties for them to turn into vices,
and encourage her to share in her husband's evil ways.
Her penchant for dainty sweetmeats became gluttony,
and she turned her volubility to false flattery and slan-
der, saying the opposite of what she really thought,
setting people against each other and deceiving her husband wherever she could. The frankness with which
she used to indulge in innocent gossip now became
brazen arrogance, and instead of submitting to her husband, she began to make him look a fool; if he resisted,
she became even more aggressive, and lost no oppor-
tunity to present herself as the true master of her
degenerate household.

Such was the tragic situation in which the two children grew up, with neither happiness in their youth
nor joyful hope for the future, since they were surrounded by nothing but strife and sorrow. Vrenchen's
position was probably the unhappier, for her mother
was dead, and, alone in the desolate house, she was at
the mercy of her barbaric and tyrannical father.

She was now sixteen, a slim, delicate girl, the curls
of her chestnut hair almost reaching down to her shining brown eyes, and the crimson of her cheeks and lips
glowing beneath her swarthy skin to give her an appearance unusual for a dark-skinned child. Every fibre in
her body quivered with life, and she was ready for
sport and play whenever the weight of her care and
suffering would lift from her mind.

But moods of depression came upon her only too

often. Not only had she to bear the grief and ever-growing misery of the family but also had to care for herself and keep herself decently dressed, although her father was reluctant to give her any money to do so. It was only with the greatest difficulty that she was able to come by a cheap Sunday dress for her slim form, or a few worthless coloured neckerchiefs. In every way she was made to feel humble and under-privileged, and at no time could she have fallen a victim to pride. In addition, she had been old enough to know how her mother had suffered, and this put a further check on her natural exuberance. Thus whenever, in spite of this, she was seen to welcome the slightest ray of sunshine that fell across her path, she presented a touching picture of innocence and charm.

At first sight Sali did not appear to be so deeply affected. He was a strong, handsome youth who could not be suspected, at least from his physical appearance, of having been ill-treated. He must have seen how disgracefully his parents were behaving, and he seemed to recall a time when things were different; indeed, he still had a clear memory of his father as an honest, wise and peaceful farmer, the same man that he now saw as a stupid greybeard, an idler and a quarreller, who raged and boasted and frittered his life away in base and foolish ventures, sliding further down the path of ruin with every step.

This angered Sali, however, and he often felt a sense of grief and shame that it should be so, although in the inexperience of youth he could not understand how things had come to this pass. Yet his worries were softened by the flattering manner in which his mother treated him, for in order to have somebody who would

stand by her in her pursuit of her evil ways, and also
to satisfy her urge to boast and swagger, she let him
have whatever he wished, bought him showy new
clothes and encouraged him to enjoy himself in whatever way he liked.

He accepted the situation with no great feeling of
gratitude, for he knew that his mother was a liar and
a gossip. He indulged his fancy with complete freedom
but took no great pleasure in doing so. Still feeling a
youth's desire for a settled and reasonably useful life, he
was as yet untainted by the evil example of his parents.
Indeed, he was almost exactly as his father had been at
that age, and as a result the latter felt a spontaneous
respect for his son, in whom, through his perplexity of
conscience, he re-lived the tortured yet cherished memory of his own childhood.

But in spite of the freedom that he enjoyed, Sali was
not really happy, realising that he had no training for
the future—for any rational pattern of work in Manz's
house had long since been abandoned. He thus found
his chief consolation in the thought of his independence and hitherto blameless conduct. Priding himself
on this, he watched sullenly as the days went by, avert-
ing his gaze from what lay in the future.

The sole obligation in his life was to continue his
father's hostility towards Marti and everything con-
nected with him. All he knew was that Marti had
offended his father and that the same enmity persisted
in Marti's house, so it was not difficult for him both to
ignore Marti and his daughter, and to play the role of
a young, if somewhat gentle antagonist himself.

Vrenchen, however, who had more to suffer than
Sali and led a far lonelier life, felt less drawn to an

attitude of rigid hostility and believed only that the well-dressed and seemingly happier Sali scorned her. She thus tried to keep out of his sight, and whenever he was close at hand, she hurried away, and he did not even bother to look in her direction. So a number of years went by without his seeing her at close quarters, and he no longer had any real idea what she looked like. Yet he often felt very curious to know, and whenever the Martis were mentioned, he involuntarily thought of the daughter whom he would now no longer recognise but whose memory was far from displeasing.

However, it was his father Manz who was the first of the two enemies to break. He was forced to leave his house; his wife had helped him squander his money, and his son had also had certain needs to fulfil, whilst Marti was the only consumer in his own tottering empire—for although his daughter was allowed to work like a slave, she was not allowed to have any wants. So, following the advice of his supporters in Seldwyla, Manz moved into the town and set himself up as an innkeeper.

It is always sad to see a farmer, accustomed to country life, move into the town with what he has salved of his possessions, and open a café or a bar, desperately trying to play the busy, genial publican while his personal feelings are anything but genial.

Only when Manz and his family moved out of their farmhouse did it become evident how poor they had become, for the dilapidated furniture which they loaded up betrayed that they had not bought or repaired anything for years. Nevertheless his wife put on her best clothes and took her place on top of the lumber-cart, already seeing herself as a town lady and looking down scornfully at her fellow villagers who peeped out from behind the hedges as the pitiful procession went by. She had made up her mind that she would captivate the whole town with her wit and charm, and that what her simpleton of a husband could not do, she would accomplish herself once she was established in a fine hostelry as the mistress of the establishment.

In fact, the hostelry turned out to be a miserable tavern in a remote and dingy little alley: the previous occupant had gone bankrupt, and the authorities were leasing it to Manz in the hope that they would thereby recoup the few hundred talers that were still outstanding. They also sold him a few casks of diluted wine and the equipment belonging to the inn—a dozen cheap bottles and glasses, and a few deal tables and benches which had once been painted red but were now badly battered and scratched. An iron ring, in which there was a carving of a hand pouring red wine from a jug into a glass, grated to and fro on a hook in front of the window, and above the front door hung a shrivelled sprig of holly.

Manz did not share his wife's complacency, and as though sensing his impending doom, he savagely whipped up the half-starved horses which he had borrowed from the new owner of his farm. His last wretched servant-boy had deserted him weeks before.

As he drove off, he saw the gloating, mocking figure of Marti pretending to busy himself with something at the roadside, and he cursed him as the sole cause of his misfortune. Sali, meanwhile, as soon as the cart was on its way, quickened his steps and went ahead, making his own way to the town through side-lanes.

'Here we are!' cried Manz, as the cart drew up in front of the dingy tavern. His wife was taken aback, for the place was a truly sorry sight. People hastened to their doors and windows to see the new farmer-turned-landlord, putting on expressions of scorn and pity in their haughty manner.

Climbing down from the cart, Manz's wife ran into the house, her eyes filling with angry tears. She had no wish to show herself again that day, for she was ashamed of the battered furniture and shabby beds which were now being unloaded. Sali was ashamed too, but was made to help his father unload their possessions in the alley, where ragged children began to climb about on the strange-looking pile and poke fun at the farmer and his downtrodden family.

The inside of the house was even more depressing, and looked for all the world like a robbers' den. The damp, dirty walls had been hastily painted with cheap lime, and apart from the dark and dingy bar-saloon with its peeling red tables, the house consisted of nothing but a few miserable little bedrooms in which, as everywhere, the previous occupants had left behind the filthiest mess imaginable.

Such was the way Manz's new life started, and such was the way it went on. During the first few weeks, particularly in the evenings, a group of neighbours might arrive who were curious to see the new landlord and whether there was any entertainment to be had there.

The landlord did not claim their attention for long: crude, graceless, boorish and unfriendly, Manz was not capable of decent behaviour, nor did he desire to be. Slowly and clumsily he filled the glasses and placed them sullenly in front of his customers, muttering a few inaudible words.

To make up for this, his wife threw herself into her task with all the more zest, and actually managed to attract a few customers for a while, though for reasons that she little guessed. She was a portly matron, and had put together a costume which she was convinced made her irresistible. This consisted of an unbleached linen skirt, a green silk spencer, a cotton apron and an untidy white ruff. She had rolled her thin hair into ridiculous little curls above her forehead and planted a large comb in the plait at the back. With a forced air of grace she waddled and floundered about, pouting stupidly in what she thought was a charming manner, tripped up to the tables with mincing gait and put down the glass or the plate of cheese, exclaiming with a smile: 'All right? Everything all right? Very good, sir! Very good, sir!' and making other stupid comments. Normally she was not at a loss for words, but now, since she was a stranger to the town, she was incapable of saying anything intelligent.

The rough townsfolk sitting there nudged each other under the table and almost exploded with laughter, holding their heads in their hands and spluttering:

'My goodness, what a creature!'

'An absolute jewel!' cried another. 'It was well worth coming here! We've not seen anything like this for ages!'

Manz observed them, glowering. Then he dug his wife in the ribs and whispered:

'You stupid fool! What do you think you're up to?'

'Leave me alone, you clumsy idiot!' she cried indignantly. 'Can't you see that I know how to get on with people? In any case, these are only rabble that you have brought in. I'll soon have better class customers in here, you'll see!'

The only light there was in the room came from a few thin tallow candles. Sali, who had heard this exchange, went out into the dark kitchen and sat down by the stove, weeping bitterly.

The guests soon tired of the spectacle of Frau Manz, and went back to places where they felt more at ease and could have a good laugh about it. Now and again a stranger might come in for a drink and stare vacantly at the bare walls around him; sometimes even a group of people arrived, raising false hopes with their jollity and excitement.

After a while the couple began to grow frightened in their gloomy house. The sun hardly ever penetrated into its rooms, and Manz, who had formerly spent half his time in the town, now began to find this confinement unbearable. When the thought of the wide, open fields came to him, he scowled morosely at the ceiling or the floor, sprang up and went to the tiny front door, only to rush back again when he saw the neighbours peering at 'the surly landlord', as they called him.

Soon they were in a state of abject poverty. In order to get anything to eat, they had to wait till someone came and paid a few coppers for a glass or two of such wine as was left; and if he asked for a sausage or something else to eat, it often cost them a great deal of trouble to obtain it. The only wine they had left was in a single large bottle which they secretly filled at another inn. They were tavern-keepers without bread or wine, trying to wear cheerful faces while having empty stomachs. Indeed, they were almost thankful

when nobody came and they could sit huddled together in the deserted saloon and drag out their pitiful
existence in a no-man's-land between life and death.

When Manz's wife finally realised the bitter truth,
she took off her green spencer, and, as she had formerly
been governed by her faults, so now, in the hour of
trial, she began to reveal her virtues. Patiently she tried
to keep up her husband's morale and instruct her son
in the ways of good living, making many sacrifices and
trying in her own way to exert a beneficient influence
which, however limited, was at least better than nothing, or than an influence of the opposite kind, and
helped to prevent things breaking up altogether. She
offered advice, to the best of her ability, on all manner
of problems, and even if her advice was useless or mis-
taken, she bore the men's anger patiently. In short, she
practised in her old age all the virtues she should have
cultivated in her youth.

In order to get some food, and also to while away
the time, Manz and his son took to fishing in the river
at places where it was permitted. This was a favourite
pastime of penniless Seldwylans. When weather conditions were favourable and the fish could be expected
to bite, dozens of men set out with rod and bucket,
and an angler would be found every few steps along
the river bank. One would be standing barefoot in the
water, wearing a long brown overcoat, another, in a
tight-fitting blue tail-coat and with an old felt hat pulled
down over one ear, would take up position in an old
willow tree. Further along there was even a man fishing in a torn floral dressing-gown—the only outer gar-

ment he possessed—with a long pipe in one hand and his fishing-rod in the other. And round the next bend a fat, bald-headed old man was standing stark naked on a stone and fishing; but although standing in the water, he had such dirty feet that it looked as if he still had his boots on.

Each man had a little jar or can full of wriggling worms which he had dug up on some previous occasion. At dusk, when the weather was sultry and the sky had clouded over, indicating the approach of rain, these characters stood in their profusion at the side of the running stream, as motionless as a row of statues of saints or prophets. The farmers drove past without heeding them, so did the boatman on the river, whose craft disturbed the water and made the anglers swear under their breath.

Twelve years earlier, when he was ploughing on the slope above the river behind his fine team of horses, Manz would have been furious if anyone had suggested that he would eventually take his place among this motley crew. He hurried round behind them and moved upstream, like some capricious shadow from the under-world seeking a cosy nook for itself by the dark waters of the infernal shades. But neither he nor his son had the patience to stand with a rod in his hand, and they recalled how the farmers used to catch fish with their hands. So, taking their rods with them as a pretence, they walked along the banks of the stream where they knew there were valuable trout to be had.

Marti's affairs, in the meantime, had also gone from bad to worse. He was bored with life, and instead of working on his neglected land, he, too, had been lured into fishing, and spent days on end splashing about in the water. Vrenchen was not allowed to leave his side, but, whatever the weather, had to carry his tackle for him through pools, streams and boggy fields, leaving all the important tasks at home undone. There was now no one left but the two of them: for since Marti only had a few acres left which he and his daughter cultivated either indifferently or not at all, he needed no help.

One evening, when storm-clouds were gathering overhead, he was walking along a deep, fast-flowing stream in which the trout were leaping high. Suddenly he saw his enemy Manz coming towards him on the other bank, and was filled with scorn and rage at the sight of him. They had not approached so close to each other for years, except in courts of law, where they had to restrain their insults, and Marti shouted out in fury:

'What are you doing here, you cur? Why don't you stay in your miserable hovel?'

'Just you wait, you blackguard!' cried Manz. 'If you're down to catching fish, it will soon be all up with you!'

The rushing of the stream grew louder, and Marti had to shout to make himself heard.

'Shut your mouth, you scoundrel!' he shrieked. 'It was you that ruined me!'

As the storm wind rose, the willows at the water's edge began to sway violently to and fro, and Manz could hardly be heard above the noise.

'I'd be only too glad if I had, you miserable wretch!' he shouted.

'You dog!' cried Marti.

'You stupid idiot!' Manz bellowed back.

Marti rushed along the bank like a wild animal and looked for a place to cross. He was the more furious of the two because he believed that, as an innkeeper, Manz must at least have had enough to eat and drink and be leading a reasonably comfortable life, whilst he, Marti, was unjustly condemned to the monotony of his broken-down farmstead.

In a fine rage himself, Manz stalked along on the opposite bank. Behind him walked Sali who, instead of listening to the angry quarrel, looked across in curiosity and surprise at Vrenchen, who was following her father and staring in shame at the ground in front of her so that her curly brown hair fell down over her face. In one hand she carried a wooden fish-bucket, while with the other she had been carrying her shoes and stockings, and holding up her skirt to keep it from getting wet. On Sali's approach she lowered it in embarrassment; yet if she had looked up, she would have seen that Sali no longer looked proud and superior, but was himself utterly downcast.

While Vrenchen fixed her eyes dejectedly on the ground, and Sali could do nothing but stare at the slim, graceful figure, neither of them noticed that the two men, who had now stopped shouting at each other, were running furiously towards a wooden bridge which had just come into view. The storm was breaking, and flashes lit up the eerie, dismal scene. The thunder began to roll through the dark grey clouds, and heavy drops of rain were falling as the men rushed on to the little bridge. As it swayed to and fro under their weight, they grabbed each other savagely and began to strike each other with their fists, their faces livid and distorted with rage.

It is not a pleasant sight to see sober-minded men brought to a point where, whether from aggressiveness, rashness or mere self-defence, they become involved in a fight against people with whom they have no real quarrel. But this is nothing in comparison with the pitiful prospect of two mature men who have known each other for years being driven by a personal hatred to lay hands on each other.

Yet such was the state to which these two ageing men had degenerated. The last time they had fought was fifty years ago; since then neither had touched the other save to shake hands as friends, and this only rarely, since they were phlegmatic and independent by nature.

After aiming a few blows at each other, they began to wrestle, snarling and groaning as they tried to throw each other over the creaking handrail into the water below. The children had now caught up with them, and Sali jumped ahead to help his father put an end to his hated enemy, who appeared to be the weaker of the two and on the verge of collapse. Vrenchen dropped everything she was carrying and rushed screaming to her father's side, holding him in her arms to protect him, but only hampering him in his struggle. The tears streamed from her eyes and she looked imploringly at Sali, who was on the point of seizing Marti and finally overpowering him.

Then, as though by instinct, he gripped his own father, trying to quieten him and get him away from his enemy. This brought a brief pause in the struggle, while all four swayed to and fro on the bridge.

As they fought to separate their parents, the two children came close to each other. At that moment a ray of sunlight glinted through a gap in the clouds, and

Sali saw before him the face that he had known so well
but which had since taken on a fresh beauty. Vrenchen
saw his astonishment, and gave him a fleeting smile
through her tears. Pitting his strength against that of
his father, Sali finally succeeded in getting him away
from Marti and persuading him to desist. When the
two men regained their breath, they turned away from
each other and began again to curse and swear. The
anxious children kept silent, but as the two groups
parted, they quickly clasped each other's hands, cold
and wet from the water and the fish, without their
parents noticing.

The clouds had now closed in again; it was getting
darker and darker, and the rain came down in torrents
as the angry farmers went their way. Manz, shivering
in the cold, trudged homeward through the dark, wet
lanes, his hands in his pockets, bowing his head before
the driving rain, and tears, which he had dared not wipe
away lest his son should notice them, trickled down
his cheeks.

But Sali saw nothing. Blissfully happy, he noticed
neither wind nor rain, neither darkness nor grief, and
felt as rich and carefree as a prince. He was haunted by
the vision of the brief smile on Vrenchen's face, and
only now, over half-an-hour later, did he return it,
giving a tender smile to the rain and the darkness, and
cherishing the thought that she could not but feel his
presence and step out of the shadows to greet him.

The following day Manz was so shaken that he would
not leave the house. His feud, added to the misery of
recent years, took on a harsher aspect and pervaded

the whole oppressive atmosphere of the shabby house.
Manz and his wife wandered listlessly and despondently
from the bar into the gloomy rooms behind, from there
into the kitchen, and from the kitchen back into the
bar, to which no customer ever came. In the end they
would each sit in a corner and pick some meaningless
quarrel, falling asleep from time to time, and waking
to the thoughts of an uneasy conscience.

But Sali saw nothing of this, for his thoughts were
only of Vrenchen. Since the events of the previous day
he had not only felt unbelievably rich but also seemed
to have experienced a sensation of indescribable beauty
and goodness. This experience had been visited upon
him from above and was the source of an unceasing
wonderment and happiness, yet he seeemed to have
been aware of it all along. Nothing can be compared
with the bliss that comes to one in human shape—a
personal shape with its own God-given name.

This day Sali felt neither idle nor unhappy, neither
poor nor abandoned. For hour after hour he tried to
conjure up in his mind the vision of Vrenchen's face,
but so feverish were his attempts that he almost lost
sight of her and began to believe that the vision would
never return. Yet she seemed to be for ever before his
eyes: he felt the warmth of her presence, and seemed
to be in the power of something that he had only seen
once and did not understand. In his happiness he could
clearly recall her features as a little girl but not those
which he had seen the day before. Had he never seen
her again, his imagination would have had to put her
picture together piece by piece until it was complete.
But now that his eyes had claimed their own joyful
role in this task, his wily imagination obstinately refused

to play its part. So as the afternoon sun streamed into the upper storeys of the dark houses, he stepped out through the door and wandered off towards his old home, which he now saw as a heavenly Jerusalem with twelve shining gates, and the closer he came to it, the faster his heart beat.

On his way he passed Vrenchen's father walking towards Seldwyla. Wild and untidy, his beard grey and unkempt, he wore the vindictive mien of one who had frittered away his own possessions and was now intent on bringing ruin upon others. Yet as he passed him, Sali felt not hatred but fear and apprehension, as though his fate rested in the hands of this old farmer, from whom he would rather have received his life as a gift than wrenched it from him as a prize.

But Marti just gave him a vicious glance and went his way. This was as Sali wished, however, for as he watched the figure moving away from him, he began to realise the true nature of his own feelings. Slipping unobtrusively through paths on the outskirts of the village, which he had known from childhood, he soon found himself in front of Marti's farmhouse.

It was years since he had seen the place from close quarters, for even while they were still living here, the rival families avoided entering each other's land. Sali stared in amazement at the desolate scene. Marti had been forced to sell his fields one by one, and there was now nothing left but the house itself and the yard in front of it, together with an area of garden and the one field by the river, to which he was obstinately clinging as long as he could. But he made no attempt at proper cultivation, and on the field where the lines of golden corn used to wave at harvest time, all manner of odd

seeds left over in bags and boxes had been planted—
turnips, cabbage and the like, together with a few potatoes. The whole impression was of a carelessly-tended
vegetable patch from which he could eke out a hand-
to-mouth existence—here a handful of turnips, there a
clump of potatoes or cabbages, and the rest left to grow
wild or to rot. People walked in or out of it at will,
and what had formerly been a fine large field was now
almost indistinguishable from the disputed strip of waste
land from which the whole tragedy stemmed.

The area round the house was no longer farmed. The
stable was empty, the door swung to and fro on one
hinge, and across the dark entrance thousands of half-
grown spiders wove their glistening webs in the sunlight. By the open door of the barn, which used to
house the rich harvest, hung some cheap fishing tackle,
the tools of Marti's poaching. Not a hen or a pigeon,
not a cat or a dog was to be seen in the yard; the only
living thing left was the fountain, but instead of flowing through the pipe, the water was seeping out through
a hole and collecting in puddles on the ground, sym-
bolising to perfection the spirit of decay.

It would not have cost Marti much effort to mend
the hole in the pipe. But Vrenchen was made to struggle
to get herself clean water from these foul conditions and
wash her clothes in the puddles instead of in the wash-
tub, which stood there cracked and dried up.

The house itself presented an equally lamentable
appearance. Many of the windows were broken and
patched up with strips of paper; yet the panes were
probably the friendliest thing about the whole melan-
choly scene, for they were all polished and spotlessly
clean, even the broken ones, and shone like Vrenchen's

own eyes, which brought to the dark, dilapidated house the only brightness that it had. And like the curly hair that surrounded her eyes, and the orange cotton neckerchiefs she wore, so the wild creeper twined its way round the shining windows and along the walls, merging with a mass of swaying beanstalks and a fragrant cluster of orange wallflowers. The beans were clinging to rakes or brooms stuck upside down in the ground, and twined round the rusty pike which Vrenchen's grandfather had used when he was a sergeant in the cavalry. More beans were growing up a battered ladder which had stood for ages against the side of the house, and were hanging down in front of the brightly-polished windows like the curls above Vrenchen's eyes.

The farmyard, now more picturesque than practical, stood somewhat apart from the neighbouring houses, and at this moment there was not a soul in sight, so without fear of being seen, Sali leaned against an old shed some distance away and looked steadily across at the silent, ramshackle building.

After a while Vrenchen appeared at the door and stared out for a long time, as though meditating. Sali stood motionless, his eyes fixed on her. At last she turned her head and saw him. They stared at each other as though they had seen a mirage. Then Sali began to walk slowly across towards her. Stretching out her arms to him, she whispered:

'Sali!'

Gazing into her eyes, he gripped her hands. As she reddened, tears sprang to her eyes.

'What do you want?' she said in low tones.

'Just to see you,' he answered. 'Let us be friends again!'

'And our parents?' she murmured, turning her tear-stained face away.

'Are we to blame for what they have done and what they have made of their lives?' he cried. 'If we two stay together and care for each other, perhaps we can make up for all the misery they have caused.'

'No good would ever come of it,' replied Vrenchen with a sigh. 'You must go your own way, Sali.'

'Are you alone?' he asked. 'May I not come in for a moment?'

'Father told me he was going into Seldwyla to teach your father a lesson. But you must not stay, because someone might see you when you leave. So please go now, while nobody is about.'

'No, I will not!' cried Sali. 'I have been thinking of you ever since yesterday, and I am not leaving until we have talked to each other at least for a little while. It will do us good!'

Vrenchen hesitated for a moment. Then she said:

'I shall have to go out to our field this evening to fetch some vegetables. You know the field I mean—it is the only one we still have. Nobody will be there, because the others are working somewhere else. Meet me there if you want to. But go away now, and be careful that no one sees you. People no longer have any dealings with us round here, but their gossip would soon reach my father's ears.'

They let go of each other's hands, only to grasp them again and exclaim with one breath:

'But how are you?'

Instead of replying, they stammered out their question again, while the answer was to be seen in the look in their eyes. As is the way with lovers, the words would not come, and half blissful, half sorrowful, they hurriedly parted.

'I will come soon!' cried Vrenchen, as Sali went away.

So he went out to the quiet ridge where the two fields lay spread out peacefully. The bright July sunshine, the white clouds billowing above the acres of ripe, waving corn, the sparkling blue river wending its way through the valley—for the first time in years everything filled him with joy instead of sadness, and he threw himself full-length in the shade of the cornfield at the edge of Marti's desolate waste and looked up happily up at the sky.

Barely a quarter of an hour had passed, during which his thoughts had been only of his childhood sweetheart, when he saw her standing in front of him, smiling down on him as he lay there. He sprang up in joy.

'Vreeli!' he cried.

Still smiling she stretched out her arms towards him, and hand in hand they walked along the side of the swaying corn down towards the river, exchanging only an occasional word. Happily they strolled back and forth, like a constellation rising and setting behind the sunlit curve of the ridge over which the straight furrows of their father's ploughs had once run.

Suddenly, as they raised their eyes from the blue cornflowers on the ground before them, they became aware of another, sinister body on the horizon of their world, a dark figure who had appeared from nowhere. Vrenchen trembled at the thought that he might have been lying in the corn, and Sali whispered, aghast:

'The Black Fiddler!'

The man striding along in front of them carried a

fiddle and a bow under his arm, and presented a wild, swarthy appearance. He was wearing a small black felt hat and a dirty black smock, and his hair and the stubble on his chin were also jet-black. His face and hands, too, looked black, for he performed all manner of menial jobs: he was a tinker by trade but also helped the charcoal-burners and tar-workers in the woods, and only took to his fiddle when there was an easy penny to be earned among the farmers who were making merry in some tavern or holding a celebration.

Sali and Vrenchen crept along behind him, hoping that he would leave the field without looking round. And it seemed that he would, for he behaved as though he had not noticed them. Some strange compulsion prevented them from venturing away from the narrow path and forced them to follow the mysterious figure right to the end of the field, where the cruel pile of stones still stood on the disputed corner of land. A mass of corn-poppies had taken root on it, making it look like a mountain on fire.

All of a sudden the Black Fiddler leapt with a single bound on to the top of the stones, turned and looked about him. The couple stopped in their tracks and looked up at him in confusion. They could not go on, because the path would have led them into the village, yet they did not want to turn back in full view of him.

Looking at them sharply, he cried:

'I know who you are! You are the children of the men who stole this field from me! I am delighted to see how prosperous you have become. I'll live to see the end of you yet, just you wait! Look at me, you poor little creatures! What do you think of my nose, eh?'

His nose was indeed a frightening sight, protruding sharply from his features like a bludgeon which had been thrown into his black, bony face. Beneath it was a small round hole for a mouth, from which came a perpetual puffing, hissing and whistling. Even his little hat contributed something to his uncanny appearance, for it was neither round nor pointed but seemed to change shape every few moments. Only the whites of his eyes could be seen as they flashed to and fro, like two rabbits darting hither and hither.

'Look at me!' he cried in an imperious tone. 'Your fathers know me well, and all the villagers recognise me as soon as they see my nose. Years ago it was announced that there was a sum of money due to the heir of this field. Twenty times I claimed it, but I have neither birth certificate nor proof of citizenship, and no one will accept the testimony of the gypsies who were present at my birth. So the time-limit expired, and I was swindled out of the money that rightfully belonged to me and with which I could have left here. I begged your fathers to confirm my claim, for their conscience must have told them that I was the true heir. But they chased me out of the house, and now they have gone to the devil themselves! Well, that's the way of the world, and I am prepared to accept it. So if you want to dance, I'll play for you!'

Whereupon he jumped down on the other side of the stones and made off towards the village, where the harvest was being brought in and the people were in high spirits.

When he had gone, the young couple sat down dejectedly on the stones, let go of each other's hands and hung their heads in sorrow. The Fiddler's words had

shaken them out of their childish trance, and as they sat
there in their misery, the rose-like hue of their life
clouded over, and their spirits became as heavy as the
stones on which they sat.

Then Vrenchen suddenly remembered the Fiddler's
strange face and nose, and could not help laughing.

'What a comical sight the poor man is! What a nose!'
she cried, and a sunny glow of merriment came into
her face, as though she had just been waiting for the
Fiddler's nose to push the clouds aside.

Sali looked at her and saw her amusement. But she
had already forgotten what caused it, and was now
smiling at Sali for his sake alone. Astonished and confused, he gazed open-mouthed into her eyes, like a
starving man who catches sight of a loaf of sweet,
white bread, and cried:

'Oh, Vreeli, how lovely you are!'

Vrenchen smiled at him all the more happily and
gave a low, attractive laugh whose musical ring sounded
to poor Sali like the call of a nightingale.

'You witch!' he cried. 'Where did you learn to laugh
like that?'

'There's no witchcraft about it,' said Vrenchen caressingly, taking his hand. 'I had been longing to laugh
like that. When I am on my own, I sometimes smile at
odd things, but it is not the same thing. But as long as I
am with you, I feel like laughing all the time. Do you
care a little for me, too?'

'Oh, Vreeli,' he cried, gazing devotedly into her eyes,
'I have never looked at another girl. I always felt
that it was you I would love some day, and you must
have always been in my thoughts, even though I never
knew it.'

'And you in mine—even more,' Vrenchen broke in. 'You had not seen me and did not know what I looked like, but I had often watched you from a distance, and sometimes even from quite close, without you knowing, so that I always knew what you looked like. Do you remember how often we used to come here as children? And the little cart? How small we were then, and how long ago it was! It makes us really old!'

'How old are you?' asked Sali, happy and delighted. 'Seventeen?'

'Seventeen and a half,' replied Vrenchen. 'And how old are you? Wait, I know—you're about twenty.'

'How do you know?'

'Never you mind!'

'Oh, go on!'

'No!'

'Oh, do tell me!'

'No. I won't!'

'All right, we'll see!'

This childish exchange led Sali to lay his hands on her, pretending to make his clumsy caresses appear like a form of punishment. Playfully defending herself, she, too, allowed the conversation to go on, which, for all its childishness, they both found so charming and amusing.

Then Sali, his spirit roused, made bold to grasp her by the hands and draw her down among the poppies. She lay there, looking up into the sun, her cheeks aglow and her lips parted, revealing two rows of shining white teeth. Her fine dark eyebrows met in the middle of her forehead, and her young breasts rose and fell as their hands, locked in confused embrace, pressed caressingly against her.

Sali's joy knew no bounds as he gazed at the beautiful slim form beside him. He knew that she was his, and he felt like a king.

'You've still got all your white teeth!' he smiled. 'Do you remember how we used to count them? Have you learnt to count now?'

'They're not the same ones, you baby!' laughed Vrenchen. 'The first ones came out long ago!'

Sali wanted to play their childish game again, but Vrenchen closed her ruby lips, sat up and began to plait a garland of poppies for her head. The broad ring of rich flowers gave the dark-skinned lass an irresistible charm, and what Sali held in his arms many would have paid dearly to have as a painting on their walls.

Then she sprang up and cried:

'My goodness, how hot it is! Here we are, sitting foolishly in the sun and getting burned. Let's go and sit in the tall corn!'

Gently they slipped into the cornfield, leaving hardly a trace of the way they had come, and built themselves a little nook among the golden ears which stretched up above their heads, cutting off the outside world except for the deep blue sky. Clasped in each other's arms, they kissed each other until they grew weary—if weariness is the word to describe those glimpses of the transience of mortal life which come to lovers in their moments of ecstasy.

They listened to the larks singing high above and tried to seek them out with their keen eyes. When they thought they glimpsed one flashing across the sun like a meteor, they rewarded each other with a kiss, always trying to outdo each other and pretending to have seen one.

'Look! Up there!' Sali would whisper. And Vrenchen whispered back:

'I can hear it but I can't see it!'

'Up there, a little to the right of that white cloud.'

And they would both stare at the heavens, their lips parted like the beaks of baby quails sitting in their nest, waiting only to press their lips together each time they imagined that they had seen another lark.

Suddenly Vrenchen drew away and said:

'So we agree that we both have a sweetheart, do we?'

'Yes,' replied Sali, smiling; 'it seems so.'

'Are you fond of your sweetheart?' asked Vrenchen. 'What does she look like? What can you tell me about her?'

'She is a lovely creature,' said Sali, 'with two brown eyes and ruby lips, and she walks on two legs. But I know as little about her mind as I do about the Pope of Rome! And what about yours?'

'He has two blue eyes and impudent lips, and he uses two strong, bold arms. But I know as little about his thoughts as I do about the Emperor of China!'

'We really know less about each other than if we had never met before,' said Sali. 'Time has made us strangers. What has been going on in that pretty little head of yours?'

'Oh, not much! All sorts of pranks occurred to me, but I was so depressed that I never carried them out.'

'You poor darling!' cried Sali. 'But you've learnt a trick or two by this time, I don't doubt!'

'If you really love me, you'll find out.'

'When you are my wife, you mean.'

This last word made her tremble, and she held him tighter, kissing him tenderly again and again. Tears

sprang to her eyes, and suddenly they both became sad
as they thought of their parents' feud and of how little
the future held for them.

'I must go now,' she said with a sigh.

They got up, and were walking out of the cornfield
when they saw Vrechen's father ahead of them. From
the moment he had met Sali in the village he had been
brooding suspiciously, with a petty curiosity born of
idleness, on what the lad could have been up to. Then
he had recalled the incident of the previous day. His
malice and lurking hatred set his thoughts in motion,
and soon his suspicions assumed definite shape. So although he had already reached the middle of the town,
he turned round and trudged back to the village
again.

When he reached the house, his daughter was nowhere to be seen. Hastening out on to the field, he
caught sight of the basket in which she collected the
vegetables; but Vrenchen herself was not in sight, and
he was scanning his neighbour's cornfield for her when
the frightened children emerged.

They stood there petrified. At first Marti, too, his
face an ashen grey, stood looking at them angrily. Then
he broke out in a fury and made to grasp Sali by the
throat. The boy evaded him and darted away, but
jumped forward again when he saw Marti seize the
trembling girl savagely, give her a cuff on the head
which sent her red garland flying, and take hold of her
hair to drag her away and beat her.

Without thinking, Sali picked up a stone, and half
in rage, half in fear of what might happen to Vrenchen,
brought it down on Marti's head. The old man stag-
gered about for a moment, then sank unconscious on

to the stones, dragging the screaming Vrenchen with him.

Sali released her hair from his grasp and helped her to her feet, then stood there like a statue, helpless and terrified.

Looking down at the motionless body, Vrenchen shuddered and clutched her pale face with her hands.

'Have you killed him?' she whispered.

Sali nodded dumbly.

'Oh, God! My father! My poor father!' she cried frantically, throwing herself on to his body and raising his head, on which there was no sign of blood.

She let it sink down again. Sali knelt on the other side, and together, in deathly silence, their hands hanging limply and nervelessly at their sides, they stared at the lifeless features. At last Sali broke the silence.

'Perhaps he's not really dead!'

Vrenchen pulled a petal from a corn-poppy and laid it on his pale lips. It stirred a little.

'He's still breathing!' she cried. 'Run to the village for help!'

As Sali jumped up and was about to run off, she stretched out her hand and beckoned him back.

'Don't come back here,' she said, 'and don't say a word about how it happened. Nobody shall ever make me tell anything either.'

Tears streamed down her face as she looked towards the poor, helpless Sali.

'Kiss me once more!' she cried. 'But no! Leave now! It is all over—over for ever! We can never marry!'

She pushed him away, and he ran blindly towards the village. On his way he met a little boy who did not know him. He told him to fetch the people nearest at hand, and described to him in detail where to take them. He then wandered off into the woods and spent the whole night roaming about there distractedly.

When morning came, he ventured out into the fields to see what had happened, and overheard from the conversation of some early passers-by that Marti was alive but unconscious, and that nobody knew, strangely enough, what had happened. On hearing this, Sali returned to the town and took refuge in the gloom and misery of his father's house.

Vrenchen kept her word. When questioned, she said only that she had found her father lying there in that state; and as he began to move and breathe more freely the next day, it was assumed that he had been drunk and struck his head on the stones, and there the matter ended. Vrenchen nursed him alone, only leaving his side to fetch medicaments from the doctor or to make herself something to eat, such as a plain soup of some kind. She lived on almost nothing, though she was awake day and night, and nobody helped her.

It was nearly six weeks before Marti regained consciousness, though he had already begun to take nourishment again and to show signs of life. But it was not the consciousness that he had known before. For as the power of speech returned to him, it became apparent that he had lost his reason. Only dimly did he recollect the past, and then as something amusing which was no real concern of his. He laughed idiotically and was for ever in high spirits; he lay in bed and poured forth all manner of incoherent thoughts and phrases, made grotesque grimaces, pulled his black woollen cap over his eyes and then down over his face, making his nose look like a coffin enveloped in a shroud.

Pale and anguish-stricken, Vrenchen listened to him patiently, shedding more tears over his present derangement than she had over his former cruelty. But when he did something particularly bizarre, she could not help laughing in spite of her grief, for her natural high spirits, now weighed down, were always ready to spring up again like a taut bow-string, only to sink back into an even profounder sense of despair. After he was able to get up, it was impossible to do anything with him at all; he behaved like a child, rummaging around the house and laughing, or sitting in the sun, poking his tongue out and making long speeches to the beans.

It was at this same time that what little remained of his property was finally disposed of, for the neglect and disorder had reached such a pitch that his house and his last field, which had both been mortgaged for some time, were now officially auctioned. The farmer who had bought Manz's two fields took advantage of Marti's sorry situation to settle once and for all the old argument over the piece of land with the stones on it. This was the *coup de grâce* for Marti, but in his deranged state he no longer understood anything of what was going on.

When the sale was over, the poor, demented Marti was sent to a public institution in the capital of the canton. The pitiful creature, who was in good health and always ready to eat, was given a good meal, then put in an ox-cart and taken to the town by a poor farmer who was on his way to sell a few sacks of potatoes there. Vrenchen sat in the cart with her father on his ride to this place of living burial.

It was a sad and bitter journey, but Vrenchen watched over her father carefully and attended to his every need; even if his antics attracted attention, and people ran after the cart as it passed through the villages, she did not look about her or become restless. At last they reached the rambling old building in the town. Its courtyards, its bright gardens and its long corridors were full of poor creatures like Marti, all dressed in white smocks and wearing stout leather caps on their bony heads.

Vrenchen watched as he too was put into this uni-form. He was as happy as a sandboy, and pranced about and sang.

'Good-day to you, gentlemen!' he cried to his new companions. 'What a splendid place you have here! Go back, Vreeli, and tell your mother that I shan't be coming home any more! I like it better here!

I heard a hedgehog barking as he crawled into the fold!
O maiden, give your kisses to the young and not the old!
The Rhine and the Danube flow into the sea;
The dark-eyed maid yonder's the right one for me!

Why don't you go, child? You look a picture of misery, and I am so happy!'

An attendant told him to be quiet and led him away to do some light work, while Vrenchen went back to the cart. Sitting down in it, she took out a piece of bread and began to eat. Then she fell asleep, and slept until the farmer came to drive back to the village.

It was dark by the time they arrived. Vrenchen went back to the house in which she had been born and in

which she had only two more days to live. For the first
time in her life she was completely alone. She lit the
fire to warm up what was left of the coffee, and sat
down by the hearth in utter desolation. She yearned to
see Sali just once more, and tormented herself with
this thought, but her grief and sadness made her yearn-
ing bitter, and this in turn only intensified her misery.

As she was sitting there, her head in her hands, a
figure came in through the open door. She looked up.

'Sali!' she cried, throwing her arms round his neck.
Then they looked at each other in alarm, and each cried
in the same breath:

'But how miserable you look!'

And indeed, the one looked as pale and haggard as
the other. Forgetting all that happened, she drew him
close to herself by the hearth and said:

'Have you been ill, or have things been bad with you
too?'

'No, I am not ill,' replied Sali. 'I am only sick with
longing for you. And there are some strange goings-on
at home: my father has invited in a lot of suspicious-
looking characters, and it looks to me as if he has taken
to harbouring thieves. That is why our tavern is so full
at the moment—until the whole affair comes to a terrible end. My mother is caught up in it as well, out of
a greedy desire to see some money coming in; she thinks
that she can put the whole disreputable business on a
proper basis by trying to keep some order in the place.
I had nothing to do with it, and besides, I just kept
thinking of you day and night. All kinds of tramps
come to our inn, so we heard every day what was hap-
pening in your family, and the news made my father
as happy as a child. We were told that your father had

been taken to the almshouse today. I knew you must be alone, so I came out to see you.'

Vrenchen poured out all her troubles to him, yet with the ease of someone relating a series of joyful events, for she was so happy to have Sali with her. She even managed to produce a bowl of warm coffee which she made him share with her.

'But what will you do,' said Sali, 'if you have to leave this house the day after tomorrow?'

'I don't know,' replied Vrenchen. 'I suppose I shall have to go and work as a maid. I cannot bear to live without you, Sali, but you can never be mine, because it was you who struck the blow that made my father insane. We could never have the peace of mind to build a life on this foundation.'

Sali gave a sigh.

'Many times,' he said, 'I was on the point of joining the army or looking for a job as a farm-hand in some far-off district, but I cannot leave while you are still here. My unhappiness seems to make my love stronger and more unbearable, and my whole life is torn apart 'in the struggle.'

Vrenchen smiled lovingly at him. They leaned back against the wall, basking in the radiant glow which outshone their sadness and proclaimed their love. And soon, sitting on the hard stones, without pillow or cushion, they slept softly and peacefully, like children in a cradle.

Dawn was already breaking when Sali awoke. Gently he tried to rouse Vrenchen, but she nestled drowsily against him and would not be wakened. Then he kissed her passionately. Opening her eyes, she cried, gazing up at him:

'Oh Sali! I was dreaming of you! I dreamt that we were dressed in our finery and dancing at our wedding, hour after hour, blissfully happy and without a care in the world. We longed to kiss each other but something kept drawing us apart—and now I see that it was you who were disturbing us! O how wonderful that you are here!'

Throwing her arms round him, she kissed him again and again.

'And what did you dream about?' she asked him, stroking his cheek.

'I dreamt that I was walking down a never-ending lane in the forest, and that you were walking ahead of me in the distance; sometimes you looked round and smiled and beckoned me on—that was all. It was the happiest moment of my life!'

As they walked together to the door, they looked at each other and began to laugh, for Vrenchen's right cheek and Sali's left, which had lain against each other as they slept, were quite red, while the other two had been made even paler than usual by the coolness of the night air. Gently they rubbed their two cold, pale cheeks together to make them as red as the others. The crisp morning air, the freshness of the dew and the tranquillity of the dawning day made them joyful and oblivious to their cares. Vrenchen in particular seemed filled with a spirit of carefree gaiety.

'Tomorrow evening,' she said, 'I shall have to leave this house and find shelter elsewhere. But before then I want to enjoy one real moment of happiness—with you. I want to dance and dance with you in my joy, for I cannot lose the vision of how we danced in my dream.'

'But I want to know where you are going to live,' said Sali. 'And I want us to dance as well, my darling. Yet where can we go?'

'Tomorrow there are two fairs not far from here,' answered Vrenchen. 'People will not know us there or take much notice of us. I will wait for you by the lake. Then we can go where we want and enjoy ourselves—just for this once!—But,' she then added sadly, 'we have no money, so it is no use.'

'Leave that to me,' said Sali. 'I'll get some.'

'But not from your father. Not that stolen money!'

'No, no! I still have my silver watch; I'll sell that.'

'I would not have you change your mind,' said Vrenchen, blushing. 'If we could not dance tomorrow, I think I would die!'

'It would be best if we could both die!' murmured Sali.

They parted with a sad embrace, smiling lovingly at each other as they thought of the following day.

'When will you come?' Vrenchen cried after him.

'At eleven o'clock, at the latest!' he called back. 'We'll eat lunch together in style!'

'Oh, yes!' she exclaimed eagerly. 'Then come at half-past ten instead!'

He had almost gone when she called him back again, with a look of sudden dejection on her face.

'We cannot go!' she cried through her tears. 'I have no Sunday shoes left. I even had to wear these old clogs to go into town yesterday!'

Sali was taken aback.

'No shoes?' he said. 'Then you must wear your clogs.'

'But I can't dance in these!'

'Then we shall have to buy some.'

'But how can we?'

'There are plenty of shoe-shops in Seldwyla, and in less than two hours I shall have the money.'

'But we can't walk around together in Seldwyla. And besides, there won't be enough money to buy shoes as well.'

'We shall have to make it enough! I will buy the shoes and bring them with me tomorrow.'

'Don't be silly! They wouldn't fit!'

'Then give me one of your old ones. No, wait a moment. I have a better idea. I'll measure your foot—that's easily done.'

'All right. I'll find a piece of string.'

She sat down again on the hearth, pulled up her skirt a little and slipped off one of her clogs, uncovering the white stockings she had been wearing since her journey the previous day. Sali knelt down and measured her foot as well as he could, taking its length and breadth, and carefully knotting the string to mark the size.

'Why, you're almost as good as a shoemaker!' she laughed, blushing and looking down at him affectionately. Sali reddened too and held her foot longer than he need have done. Drawing it away with an even deeper blush, she embraced the embarrassed Sali again, kissed him impulsively and then told him to go.

As soon as he reached the town, he took his watch to a jeweller, who gave him between six and seven florins for it, and a few more for the silver chain. He now felt rich, for never before had he had so much money in his possession. If only today were over and Sunday already here, he thought to himself, so that he could buy the happiness that he wanted that day to bring; and the sinister shadow of the future only added a strange lustre to the longed-for pleasures of the morrow.

The rest of the day he spent in looking for a pair of shoes for Vrenchen. It was the most delightful task he had ever undertaken. He went from one shop to another asking to see all the ladies' shoes they had, until he finally decided on a dainty pair far prettier than Vrenchen had ever worn. He hid them under his jacket and did not let go of them for a single moment during the rest of the day. He even took them to bed with him and put them under his pillow.

As he had been with Vrenchen that morning, and knew that he would see her again the next day, he slept soundly and peacefully. When dawn came, he rose happily and began to brush and clean his shabby Sunday clothes as best he could.

His mother, noticing this in surprise, asked him where he was going, for he had not taken such care over his appearance for many a day. Sali replied that he wanted to go out and see something of the world: it would ruin his health to have to stay in the house all the time.

'What sort of life is that,' grumbled his father, 'wandering about aimlessly?'

'Let the boy go,' retorted his mother. 'It may do him good. Just look what a picture of misery he is!'

'Have you got any money?' asked Manz. 'And if so, where did you get it?'

'I don't need any,' answered Sali.

'Here's a florin,' said his father, throwing it across

to him. 'Go and spend it in the inn, so that people don't think we're hard up.'

'I'm not going to the village, so you can keep the money!'

'It would be wasted on you anyway, you pig-headed fool!' cried Manz, thrusting the florin back into his pocket.

But Sali's mother, who did not know why she should feel so despondent and so concerned about her son that morning, gave him a large black neckerchief with a red border which she had hardly ever worn but which the boy had always wanted. He wound it round his neck and let the long ends hang down; then, for the first time in his life, instead of turning his collar down, he turned it right up to his ears like a man of the world. So, shortly after seven o'clock, he set out in manly pride, carrying Vrenchen's shoes in the inner pocket of his jacket.

At that moment he felt a strange urge to stretch out his hand to his father and mother as he left, and when he was out on the road he looked back at the house once more.

'Do you know what I think?' said Manz. 'He's chasing after some girl or other. That would be the last straw!'

'Perhaps he will find happiness with her,' said his wife. 'If he did, it would be wonderful for the poor boy.'

'Oh, wonderful,' sneered Manz. 'If he has the misfortune to get hold of the sort of chatterbox I've got, it will certainly be wonderful for the poor wretch!'

At first Sali made for the river, where he had arranged to meet Vrenchen, but on the way he changed

his mind and went straight to her house, for he felt he
could not wait till the appointed hour. 'Why worry
what people will say?' he thought to himself. 'I'm an
upright fellow and afraid of no one. Besides, nobody
has ever lifted a finger to help us.'

So without further ado he opened Vrenchen's door.
To his surprise he found her sitting there fully-dressed
in her finest clothes, waiting only for her shoes. When
he saw her, he stopped in his tracks and stared at her
open-mouthed, so lovely did she look. Her slim form
was sheathed in a simple blue cotton dress, fresh and
fragrant, and round her neck she wore a kerchief of
snow-white muslin. Her brown locks, usually so dis-
hevelled, were neatly combed. She had scarcely been
outside the house for weeks, and her complexion had
become even paler than before, as though from sorrow.
But this pallor now gave way to the flush of love and
joy, and on her dress she wore a beautiful spray of
rosemary, asters and roses.

She had been sitting by the open window, revelling
in the fresh, sunlit morning air. When she caught sight
of Sali, she stretched out her soft, bare arms towards
him and cried:

'How happy I am that you have come so early! Have
you really brought the shoes? I shan't stand up until
I've got them on!'

He took the cherished present from his pocket and
gave it to her. She kicked off her old clogs and eagerly
slipped into the new ones. They fitted perfectly. She
got up from her chair to see how they felt, and walked
delightedly up and down a few times. Then she drew
her long blue dress up a little and looked admiringly
at the red woollen bows which graced the new shoes,

while Sali could not take his eyes off the charming figure tripping joyfully and excitedly to and fro.

'Are you looking at my posy?' she said. 'Isn't it pretty? They were the last flowers I could find in the wilderness outside. There was a rose growing in one place, and an aster in another; and now that they're tied together, nobody could ever tell that they came from such a barren waste. So now that there is not a flower left, and the house is empty, it is time for me to leave.'

Sali looked round and noticed for the first time that all the furniture had gone.

'Poor Vreeli!' he murmured. 'Have they taken everything?'

'Yesterday they took everything they could,' she replied, 'and did not even want to leave me my bed. But now I've sold that too and got some money of my own. Look!'

And she took a few shining talers from the pocket of her dress and showed them to him.

'The man from the orphanage who was here,' she went on, 'told me to take them and start looking for a job in the town straight away.'

'But there is not a single thing left,' said Sali, who had looked into the kitchen, 'not a stick of wood, not a saucepan, not a single knife. Did you not have any breakfast?'

'No,' answered Vrenchen. 'I could have fetched something but then I thought it would be better to stay hungry so that I could eat a big meal when we go out together. How happy I am going to be today!'

'And how happy *I* would be if I could only touch you, you lovely creature!' cried Sali.

'You would only spoil my dress! And if we can spare my little posy for a while, it will make up for the way you ruffle my hair.'

'Let's be on our way, then!'

'No, we must wait until they come to fetch the bed. When they have left, I shall shut the door on the empty house and never come back. The woman who bought the bed can look after my few things.'

They sat down opposite each other and waited.

The woman soon arrived, a buxom matron with a loud voice; with her came a lad who was to carry the bedstead. When she saw Vrenchen sitting there in her finery, she gaped at the couple wide-eyed, planted her hands on her hips and exclaimed:

'Well, well, Vreeli! You're doing things in grand style—dressed like a princess, and with a friend, too!'

'You're right!' replied Vrenchen with a smile. 'And do you know who he is?'

'He looks to me like Sali Manz. "East and West shall never meet", says the proverb—but with people it's different! Yet take heed, child, and remember what happened to your fathers.'

'Oh, all that belongs to the past,' answered the smiling Vrenchen in a friendly, almost condescending tone. 'You see, Sali is my fiancé.'

'Your fiancé? Well, well!'

'Yes, and he is a rich man, too. He has just won a hundred thousand florins in the sweepstake. Just think of that!'

'A hundred thousand florins!' cried the woman, giving a violent start and clapping her hands together in amazement.

'A hundred thousand florins!' repeated Vrenchen gravely.

'Heavens above! I don't believe you, child. You're telling tales!'

'You can believe what you like!'

'But even if it is true, and you do marry him, what will you do with the money? Are you really going to live like a lady of rank?'

'Of course I am! The wedding will be in three weeks!'

'You're making it all up, you deceitful girl!'

'He has already bought a magnificent house in Seldwyla with a big garden and a vineyard. You must come and visit us when we have settled in!'

'What stories you do tell!'

'You'll see how beautiful it is. I'll make you some fine coffee and offer you sweet rolls with butter and honey.'

'Then I'll certainly come!' cried the woman, her eyes glinting greedily and her mouth watering.

'And if you come at midday on your way back from the market, there will be some strong broth and a glass of wine waiting for you!'

'That's just what I would like!'

'And I shan't forget to give you some crisp rolls and other titbits for your children.'

'I can hardly wait!'

'If you have an hour to spare, you can rummage through my chest and cases. You are sure to find a pretty neckerchief, or a piece of silk, or a bright ribbon to decorate your skirt, or a piece of material for a new apron.'

The woman danced with delight, swinging her skirts round and round.

'And if your husband needs money to buy a piece of land or some cattle, you know where to come. My dear Sali will always be pleased to invest his money profitably, and I am sure to have my own private fund for helping my intimate friends.'

The woman was by now completely won over, and said affectionately:

'I always said that you were a good, kind girl! The Lord bless you for your generosity!'

'But in return I want you to be kind to me.'

'Of course I will!'

'And to offer all your produce, whether it be fruit, potatoes or vegetables, first to me before you go to market, so that I can be sure of having a farmer I can rely on. I shall pay you as much as the others—you know that. There is nothing finer than a true friendship between a rich townswoman in her lonely villa and an upright countrywoman versed in the practical affairs of life. Many are the times when one welcomes such a friendship—in joy and suffering, at christenings and weddings, when the children go to school and are confirmed, when they embark on their apprenticeship and leave home, and in times of drought and flood, fire and hailstorm—from which God preserve us!'

'May God preserve us!' sobbed the woman, drying her eyes with her apron. 'How wise and understanding you are! Happiness will surely come your way, or there is no justice in the world! You are beautiful and intelligent, and gifted in all manner of ways. I know no finer or nobler person anywhere, and the man that wins you will feel that he is living in paradise. If he doesn't, I'll give the rogue a piece of my mind! Do you hear what I say, Sali? Be nice to my Vreeli, or I'll teach you a lesson—lucky fellow that you are, to win such a prize!'

'Then take this bundle you promised to keep until I send for it. I may even come in my carriage to collect it in person, if you have no objection. I'll bring an almond-cake with me, and you're sure to offer me a jug of milk in return.'

'Lord have mercy! Give me the bundle!'

Vrenchen took the long sack into which she had stuffed her worthless possessions, and put it on top of the rolled-up mattress which the woman was already balancing on her head, so that it looked like a tottering pillar.

'It's almost too heavy,' she said. 'Can I come back for the rest?'

'No, no,' said Vrenchen hastily, 'we must leave at once, for we have a long journey ahead of us. We have got to visit some fine relations who have suddenly appeared on the scene since we have become rich. You know what people are.'

'I do, indeed! God bless you—and think of me sometimes in your prosperity.'

Keeping her balance with difficulty, the bundle on her head, she left, followed by the lad carrying Vrenchen's once brightly-painted bed; the top, with its pattern of faded stars, he rested on his head, grasping the finely carved front posts like a Samson. Vrenchen leaned against Sali and watched the procession go on its way. Catching a last glimpse of it as it passed by the garden, looking like a moving temple, she said:

'That would make a nice little chalet or pavilion if we put it in a garden with a little table and a bench,

and planted convolvuluses around it. Would you sit
there with me, Sali?'

'Yes, Vreeli, especially when the convolvulus had
grown tall!'

'What are we waiting for? There is nothing more to
keep us here. Let us lock the house and go!'

'Who will keep the key?'

Vrenchen looked around her.

'We'll hang it on the old halberd. Father often used
to say that it had been in the house for over a hundred
years, and now it's standing guard like the last sentry!'

They hung a rusty housekey on a protruding piece
of the rusty old weapon round which the beanstalks
were twined, and left. Vrenchen went a little pale and
held her hand to her eyes, and Sali had to lead her a
little way. But she did not look back.

'Where shall we go first?' she asked.

'Let's walk out into the country,' answered Sali,
'where we can be happy all day. We have no need to
hurry. Then towards evening we'll find somewhere to
dance.'

'So we can be together the whole day and go where-
ever we like!' cried Vrenchen. '—But I'm beginning to
feel faint. Let's go first and have breakfast in some other
village.'

'All right,' said Sali, 'we'll get out of this place as
quickly as we can.'

Soon they were in open country, walking side by
side through the meadows. It was a beautiful Sunday
morning in September, not a cloud in the sky, and a
soft haze hung over the hills and woods, giving the
scene a solemn, mysterious atmosphere. The sound of
church bells came from all quarters—on one side a deep,

melodious chime from a rich village, on another two tinkling little bells from a poor parish. The lovers, resplendent in their finest clothes, did not think of what the end of the day would bring but surrendered themselves to the silent joy of the moment, roaming freely in the sunshine like a couple who were made for each other. Every sound or call that was heard in the stillness of that Sunday morning echoed in their souls, for love is like a bell which vibrates to the faintest, most distant sound and gives out its own special music.

Although they were hungry, the half-hour's walk to the next village seemed only a stone's throw, and shyly they entered the first inn they came to.

Sali ordered a large breakfast, and while it was being prepared, they sat quietly and watched the comings and goings in the light and roomy parlour.

The landlord was also a baker, and the pleasant smell of fresh-baked bread filled the whole house; baskets full of all kinds of bread were brought in, for after church the villagers used to come here to collect their white loaves or have their morning drink. The landlord's wife, a fine, handsome woman, was quietly and smilingly dressing her children, and when one of the little girls was ready, she ran across to Vrenchen, showed her how beautiful she looked and confided to her all her proud and happy secrets.

When the coffee was brought, strong and with a fine aroma, the young couple took their places hesitantly at the table, as though they were guests of the house. Soon, however, they began to feel more confident, and to whisper softly and happily to each other. Vrenchen was in raptures over the rich coffee, the thick cream,

the warm rolls, the fresh butter and honey, the pan-
cakes and all the other delicacies.

But her greatest joy came from seeing Sali beside
her, and she ate with the eagerness of one who had been
fasting for a whole year. The fine china and the silver
coffee-spoons, too, filled her with delight. The landlord's wife obviously considered them to be honest
young folk who deserved to be treated with respect,
and from time to time she sat down at their table and
chatted to them, taking pleasure in their sympathetic
conversation.

Vrenchen was so enchanted that she did not know
whether she would rather go out into the countryside
to roam with her sweetheart through the woods and
meadows, or stay in the friendly inn so as to preserve
the illusion, at least for a few hours, that the fine house
was really hers. But Sali made the decision for her by
declaring firmly that they had better be on their way,
giving the impression that they had an important
journey to make. The landlord and his wife accompanied them to the door, and although their poverty
could not be disguised, they had displayed a
perfect demeanour, and the host bade them a friendly
farewell.

Courteously the young couple took their leave and
walked out into the sunshine. Lost in dreams, and with
no thought of their family strife and misery, they wandered side by side through the thick oak woods like
the children of good, honourable parents. Vrenchen
walked demurely along the damp, slippery path, her
head bowed, her hands folded gracefully in front of
her; Sali, however, held himself erect and stepped out
boldly and purposefully, his eyes fixed on the trees

around him like a woodman deciding which ones could most profitably be felled.

At last they awoke from their day-dreaming, looked at each other and, seeing that they both still wore the same expression as when they left the inn, went red and hung their heads in embarrassment. But youth is care-free; the woods were green, the sky was blue—they were alone together again, and happiness returned to them once more.

But they did not remain alone for long, for the road began to fill with young couples and cheerful groups of friends, jesting and singing on their way home from church. Country-folk have their favourite walks just like townspeople, but the parks where country-folk go cost nothing to maintain, and are more beautiful as well. The countryman does not walk through his flowering fields with a special 'Sunday-morning' mentality but strolls along lonely paths through copses and by green hill-tops, resting by the verge of the forest or at the top of a grassy slope from which he can look out over the surrounding countryside, singing cheerfully and absorbing the unspoiled beauties of nature as he goes.

And since he does not do this as a penance but as a pleasure, he must have a feeling for nature which goes far beyond considerations of practical value. Just like the old women who seek the paths along which they wandered as children, so young boys break off green twigs as they go. Even a rugged farmer in the prime of life takes delight in cutting a cane when his way takes him through the woods, paring off the leaves until only a green tuft is left at the top; bearing it aloft like a sceptre, he takes it with him into whatever office he visits, stands it solemnly in a corner, and invariably remembers to collect it again when he leaves, however serious his business has been; he carries it home in perfect condition and gives it to his youngest son, who is the only one permitted to break it.

When Sali and Vrenchen saw the strangers coming, they smiled to themselves and rejoiced in the thought that they, too, formed a couple. They left the road and slipped into the wood, following narrow lanes that led into silence and solitude, stopping where their fancy took them, then running off again. Their minds were as unclouded as the sky above them; they were oblivious to where they had come from and where they were going.

For all their excitement and their running to and fro, Vrenchen still looked as fresh and charming as in the early morning, while Sali had acted, not like a country bumpkin of twenty, the son of a dissolute tavern-keeper, but like a youth of good family, and there was something almost comic in the tenderness, the care and the reverence which he lavished on his radiant companion. For on this, the one day granted to them, they had to live through all the moods of love, to capture the lost serenity of days gone by, and to fill the moments that were left to them before the hour of their final sacrifice.

As they walked, they grew hungry again. Then from the top of a shady hill they saw a village nestling below in the sunshine, and decided to have lunch there. They hastened down the hill and entered the village, walking with the same modest air as when they had left the previous village. There was nobody to recognise them. Vrenchen in particular had hardly mixed with people at all in recent years, still less had she been to other villages. They thus passed for a pleasant, respectable young couple out for a walk.

They stopped at the first inn, and Sali ordered a substantial meal. A special table was decked for them, and as they sat there quietly and unassumingly, they looked at the fine walnut panelling, the walnut dresser, simple but well-polished, and the snow-white curtains.

The landlord's wife came up to them in a friendly manner and put a vase of fresh flowers on the table.

'You can feast your eyes on these till the soup comes!' she said with a smile. 'And if I might make so bold as to ask—are you not a young couple on your way to the town to get married?'

Vrenchen blushed and was too embarrassed to raise her eyes. Sali kept silent too, and the woman continued:

'Well, you're both still young! Youthful wed eats happy bread, as the saying goes; and you are an attractive and honest-looking pair, so you need not be ashamed. A decent couple can make a success of life if they start young, and work hard, and are faithful to each other—and *that* you must certainly be, for you have many years before you. If you husband them well, they can be happy years. But don't mind me, young people. It's just that I was so pleased to see such a handsome couple!'

The maidservant brought the soup, and as she had overheard part of the conversation and had always hoped to get married herself, she looked jealously at Vrenchen, envious of the happiness that seemed to be in store for her. Back in the serving-room she gave vent to her ill-temper.

'They are another of those vagabond couples without a penny to their name,' she said to the landlord's wife

in a voice loud enough for all to hear; 'they have no
friends, no dowry, nothing but the prospect of poverty
and beggary, yet they rush into the town to celebrate
their wedding! Where shall we be if young things like
that get married, when they can't even tie their own
apron-strings or make a proper soup? I'm really sorry
for the boy—he's come to a pretty pass with his young
Dulcinea!'

'Hold your tongue, you spiteful hussy!' hissed the
wife. 'I am not going to see any harm come to them.
They seem a perfectly decent couple from the hills—
they're probably mill-hands. Their clothes are shabby
but clean, and as long as they love each other and work
hard, they will go further than you with your mali-
cious gossip. If you can't control your tongue, nobody
is likely to propose to you—you surly creature!'

Thus Vrenchen experienced all that befalls a bride
going to her wedding: the sympathy of an understanding woman; the jealousy of an old maid who both
praises and pities the bridegroom out of personal spite,
because she herself dearly wants to marry; and a delici-
ous repast at the side of the bridegroom himself. Her
cheeks bore the flush of a red carnation and her heart
was thumping, but she ate and drank with enthusiasm
and continued to be polite to the maidservant, though
she could not resist casting affectionate glances at Sali
and whispering to him, which only made the poor
youth more embarrassed.

For a long time they sat there happily, as though
reluctant to break the blissful spell. The innkeeper's
wife brought them some pastries for dessert, and Sali
ordered a stronger wine to go with them, which sent
Vrenchen's blood coursing through her veins; she took

only occasional sips, however, and sat there shyly and demurely, like a real bride. She played this role partly out of a rouguish desire to see whether she really could act the part, and partly because she truly felt like a bride. As she sat there, held in the grip of both love and fear, the walls of the room seemed to close in on her, and she made Sali take her out into the open air again.

Instinctively they seemed to avoid returning to the side-lanes where they would be alone, and silently they walked along the road, past the groups of people standing there, looking to neither left nor right.

When they had left the last house behind them and were on the way to the next village, in which the fair was being held, Vrenchen caught Sali's arm and said in a trembling whisper:

'Sali, why should we not give ourselves to each other and be happy?'

'I do not know why,' he stammered, gazing at the soft September sunshine which covered the meadows, and struggling to control his emotions. They stopped to kiss each other, but a party of young folk came into view, and they parted and walked on.

The big village was already swarming with activity. The sound of festive music came from the stately inn, and the young villagers had started to dance, while in the square a few stalls had been set up, with pastries and sweets and cheap trinkets. The children were crowding around, together with others who had come rather to look than to buy.

Sali and Vrenchen went over to look as well, each with the wish to buy something for the other, since this was the first time that they had been to a fair together. Sali bought a big gingerbread house covered in gleam-

ing white icing, with white doves sitting on its green
roof and a little Cupid peeping out of the chimney,
pretending to be a sweep; chubby-cheeked figures embraced each other at the open windows, their tiny red
lips joined in a real kiss, since the painter had in his
haste made only a single red daub for their two mouths.
Their eyes were little black spots, and on the red door
were inscribed the following lines:

> 'Come into my house, my darling!
>   Yet know, my dearest friend,
> That kisses are the currency
>   That people here must spend.'

> The maiden spake: 'My hero,
>   I have no trace of fear!
> My only thought is of the joys
>   That we can savour here!

> And this it was that drew me,
>   To seek here thy embrace!'
> So come, good lovers, follow now
>   The custom of this place!

Painted on the walls of the house, to the left and right
of the door, were a gentleman in a blue cloak and a
fine lady with a very large bosom, and in the spirit of
the poem each was inviting the other inside.

For Sali, Vrenchen bought a heart, on one side of
which was a slip of paper with the words:

An almond sweet is buried in this heart so gay and
free;
But sweeter than the almond is the love I bear to thee!

On the other side was the inscription:

And when this heart is eaten, recall the words I say:
My love will live unsullied until the Judgement Day!

Eagerly they read these mottoes, and never did a
poem strike so deep, or was adjudged so beautiful, as
was this gingerbread doggerel. It seemed to have been
written especially for them, so exactly did it mirror
their own feelings.

'You have given me a home,' said Vrenchen with a
sigh. 'And I have given you one, too—a true one. For
our hearts are now our home, and we are carrying it
about with us like the snails!'

'Then we are like two snails carrying each other's
home!' smiled Sali.

'All the more reason why we should stay close together, so that each can be near his own!'

Not realising that their jests were of the same kind
as those of the many gingerbread shapes laid out before
them, they continued to examine the sentimental in-
scriptions, particularly those attached to the lavishly
decorated hearts, large and small, that lay there. Vrenchen discovered a gilded heart strung like a lyre, on
which was written:

Soft music in this heart abounds;
The more you play it, the more it sounds!

And when she read this, she seemed to hear the sound
of music in her own heart.

Then they found a portrait of Napoleon which bore
the following motto:

Napoleon was a hero real,
With heart of oak and sword of steel.
My love is fair and fancy free,
Yet faithful she will ever be!

While pretending to be absorbed in reading such
verses, they each made secret purchases: Sali bought a
gilt ring with a green stone, and Vrenchen chose a black
chamois ring crowned with a golden forget-me-not.
They both seemed to be urged by the thought to give
each other some little trinket when the hour of their
parting came. So engrossed were they in what they
were doing that they did not notice the people gradually gathering round them in curiosity. A number of
girls and lads from their own village were there and
formed a circle round them, struck by their Sunday
clothes, but the young couple seemed totally oblivious
to the outside world.

'Just look!' said a voice. 'It's Vrenchen Marti with
that young Sali from the town! See how attached they
are to each other, how affectionate and devoted! I wonder where they're going?'

The bystanders' surprise sprang from a strange
mixture of pity, contempt for the baseness and
depravity of their parents, and envy of the young
couple's happiness; for the pure love which they
cherished for each other set them as far apart from
the common mass as had their former loneliness and
poverty.

Awaking at last from their reveries, they looked
round them and saw the staring faces. No one greeted
them, nor did they know whether they should greet
the others—though this unfriendliness and mutual dis-
trust were more the product of their embarrassment
than a feeling of deliberate hostility.

Poor Vrenchen trembled and turned pale, but Sali
led her away, and holding her little house in her hand,
she followed him, although the cheerful sound of the

band was coming from the inn and she longed so much to dance.

'We cannot dance here,' said Sali, when they had moved some distance away.

'Then let us give up our plans, and I will try to find somewhere to stay for the night.'

'No!' cried Sali. 'You shall have your dance! That's why I bought the shoes! Let's go and join the poor folk; that's where we really belong, and they won't look down on us there. People always dance in the Garden of Paradise when the fair is here, because it belongs to the same parish, so let's go there. They might even give you a bed.'

Vrenchen shuddered at the thought of sleeping for the first time in a strange place but involuntarily she followed her guide, who was now all she had in the world.

The 'Garden of Paradise' was an inn beautifully set on a lonely hillside, with a wide view of the surrounding country, but it was only frequented by the lower classes, children of poor farmers and labourers, and all kinds of vagabonds. It had been built a hundred years ago by a rich eccentric as a small country house, but after he died, nobody wanted to live there. Since it could not be put to any useful purpose, the whole estate fell into decay and finally passed into the hands of a man who turned it into an inn. The appearance of the place, however, together with its name, remained unchanged.

It consisted of a single-storeyed building with a terrace on the roof, the sides of which were open and the roof supported by four weatherbeaten sandstone pillars, one at each corner, depicting the four archangels. The portico was adorned with little cherubs, also carved in

sandstone, with big heads and fat bodies, playing tri-
angles, fiddles, pipes, cymbals and tambourines. These
instruments had originally been painted gold, and the
ceiling inside, as well as the outer walls of the whole
building, were covered with faded frescoes depicting
merry groups of angels and figures of singing, dancing
saints. But everything was pale and blurred as in a
dream, and vines now covered the whole surface, with
dark grapes ripening in the midst of the thick foliage.
The house was surrounded by large, untended chestnut trees, and gnarled rose trees sprawled over the
ground like elderberry bushes.

The terrace was used for dancing, and from a long
way off Sali and Vrenchen could see the figures up
there, while crowds of revellers drank and jostled each
other round the house below. Vrenchen, who was still
reverently carrying her gingerbread house, looked like
one of those religious benefactresses in old pictures,
who bear in their hands a model of the church or nun-
nery which they have founded. But the house that was
in Vrenchen's mind would never be built.

When she heard the cheerful dance-music, however,
she forgot her sorrows and wanted nothing but to
dance with Sali. Threading their way through the
people sitting in front of the inn and in the parlour,
poor, ragged folk from Seldwyla and surrounding
places who were looking for a cheap day's entertainment, they climbed the stairs and began to dance a
waltz, gazing silently into each others' eyes.

When the waltz had ended, they looked round them.
Vrenchen's little house was crushed, and she was just
preparing to cry, when she looked up to see the sinister
figure of the Black Fiddler.

He was sitting perched on a bench on top of a table, and looked as black as ever, but this time he had stuck a sprig of green pine-needles in his hat, while at his feet stood a bottle of red wine and a glass. Yet although he stamped his feet the whole time he was playing his fiddle, he never knocked the bottle or glass over, so that the whole performance was like a step-dance. By his side sat a handsome but sad-looking young man with a horn, and a hunchback with a double-bass.

Sali, too, shrank from the sight of the Fiddler, who, however, greeted them cordially and cried:

'I knew I would play a tune for you to dance to some day! So enjoy yourselves, young lovers, and let us drink to one another!'

He held out the glass to Sali, who took it and drank his health. When the Fiddler saw how frightened Vrenchen looked, he tried to console her, and succeeded in making her smile at some of his good-natured jests. Slowly her cheerfulness returned, and they were glad to have a friend there; indeed, they almost felt as though they were under the Fiddler's special care and protection.

On and on they danced, forgetting both themselves and the world in the singing and rejoicing around them, that rang out far into the countryside as the silver haze of the autumn evening began to settle. They danced until darkness fell and most of the merry guests had dispersed to their distant homes, singing and shouting.

Those who stayed were the real fraternity of the road, who were set on following a joyful day with a joyful night. Among them were some motley-dressed characters who appeared to know the Fiddler well, such as a young lad in a green corduroy jacket and a crump-

led straw hat round which he had twined a garland of
mountain-ash leaves. This boy had with him a wild-
looking girl in a cherry-red cotton skirt with white
spots, who had set on her head a coronet of vines, with
a cluster of grapes over each temple. This couple was
the most abandoned of all those present, darting from
one corner to another, and dancing and singing without pause.

A slim, attractive girl was also there, dressed in a
faded black silk dress and with a white linen scarf on
her head, the long point hanging down at the back; the
red stripes woven into it showed that it had been a
towel or a serviette. Beneath this head-covering glistened a pair of deep blue eyes. Round her neck ond on
her breast hung a necklace, not of coral but of six
rows of mountain-ash berries threaded on a string. The
whole evening she danced alone, invariably turning
down the young men's offers. Lightly and gracefully
she tripped round the room, smiling each time she
passed the sad-looking horn-player, who looked the
other way whenever she approached. Other young
women were also there with their consorts, all shabbily
dressed but no less friendly and merry for that.

When darkness fell, the landlord refused to light the
candles, claiming that the wind would only blow them
out; besides, he said, the full moon would soon be up,
and moonlight was quite sufficient illumination for the
money that they had spent. This decision met with
universal approval, and the company took up position
on the parapet, watching the red glow that was already
visible on the horizon.

As soon as the moon's rays fell on the open dance-
floor, the couples began to dance again, this time gently

and in blissful happiness, as though they were dancing by the glow of a thousand candles. The strange light seemed to bring them closer together, and in the general merriment Sali and Vrenchen could not but join in and dance with other partners. Yet whenever they were drawn apart for a while, they quickly sought each other again and rejoiced as though they had not seen each other for years.

Whenever he had to dance with another girl, Sali looked depressed and ill-tempered, and kept looking round for Vrenchen. But she did not look at him as she swept past, and, her cheeks flushed like a rose, seemed happy to dance with any partner.

'Are you jealous, Sali?' she asked, when the musicians had become tired and stopped playing for a while.

'Heaven forbid!' he replied. 'How could I be?'

'Then why do you look so cross when I dance with other boys?'

'It's not your dancing with other boys, but my having to dance with other girls! I feel as though I'm holding a piece of wood in my arms! Don't you feel the same way?'

'Oh, I'm always happy when I'm dancing, as long as I know that you are there too. But if you ever went away and left me alone, I think I would die!'

They went down the stairs and stood in front of the inn. Vrenchen threw her arms around him and clasped him to her slender, trembling body, laying her flushed, tear-stained cheek against his.

'We cannot stay together,' she sobbed, 'yet I cannot leave your side, even for a single moment.'

Sali held her tightly in his arms and covered her with kisses. Desperately he tried to think of an answer but he could find none. For even had he been able to outlive the despair and unhappiness which attended his own life, his inexperience and his youthful passion ill equipped him to face a long testing-time of renunciation. And there also remained the figure of Vrenchen's father, whom he had rendered helpless for the rest of his life.

They both knew that they could only find true happiness by becoming man and wife. Lonely and abandoned as they were, this thought was the last flicker of that flame of honour which had burned in their families in times gone by, and which their ambitious fathers had extinguished when, thinking to augment this honour by adding to their material wealth, they had so recklessly laid hands on the property of another.

Such events happen every day, but from time to time fate decides to intervene, and brings together two such seekers after fame and riches, letting them provoke and finally devour each other like wild beasts. For it is not only kings and emperors who miscalculate this way: men from the humblest cottages can be equally guilty, showing through their erring ways that the obverse of a badge of honour is a badge of shame.

Sali and Vrenchen, however, remembered how their families had once enjoyed honour and esteem, and how they had been brought up as the children of trusted and respected fathers. Then they had been drawn apart, and when they finally came together again, they saw in each other that happiness which their families had lost, and their memories made them cling all the more passionately to each other; the happiness they craved had to have a firm foundation, and though their blood throbbed through their veins, urging them to consummate their union, that foundation seemed to be ever beyond their grasp.

'It's dark now,' said Vrenchen, 'and we must part.'

'Do you think I will leave you here alone?' cried Sali. 'No, never!'

'But it will be no easier when tomorrow comes.'

'Let me give you a piece of advice, you young simpletons!' came a harsh voice from behind them—and the Fiddler stepped out of the shadows.

'There you stand,' he went on, 'wanting to be united but not knowing which way to turn. My advice is, take each other as you are and have done with it. Come into the mountains with me and my friends. You won't need a parson there, or money, or a licence, or honour, or a marriage-bed—nothing but your own desires. Things are not at all bad where we live: the air is healthy, and there is plenty to eat if you are prepared to work. The green woods are our home, and there we live and love as we please; and in winter we either make ourselves a warm resting-place or hide in the farmer's hay-loft. So make up your minds! Call this your wedding-day and come with us, then you'll be rid of all your troubles! You can live happily ever after—or anyway for as long as you have a mind to. People reach a ripe old age in the freedom which we enjoy, believe me!—And don't think,' he continued, 'that I bear you any ill-will for what your parents did to me. I won't deny that it gives me a certain satisfaction to see that you have come to this pass, but I am content to leave it at that. You are welcome to join us. And if you decide to do so, I will do my best to help you.'

His manner became friendlier as he said this.

'Well, think it over for a while,' he concluded, 'but if you take my advice, you'll come along with us. Forget the world, be married and turn your back on the others! Think of the bridal chamber waiting for you in the depths of the forest—or in a haystack, if it's too cold!'

He went into the inn. Holding the trembling Vrenchen in his arms, Sali said:

'What shall we do? Why not let the world go its way, and love each other fully and freely?'

But he said it more as a despairing jest than in earnest, and Vrenchen, kissing him, replied with a childlike simplicity:

'No, that is not the way I want things to be. The young horn-player and the girl in the silk dress took that way out, they say, and were deeply in love; last week she was unfaithful to him for the first time, but he could not get over it, and now he is sullen and refuses to speak either to her or to anyone else, and the others all laugh at him. As a form of mock penance she dances by herself and will not talk, thus ridiculing him still further. You can see from the poor boy's face that he will make it up with her before the day is out, but I do not want to live where things like this go on. I would give anything to call you mine, and I could not bear the thought of being unfaithful to you.'

Her body quivered as she pressed herself against him. Ever since leaving the inn that afternoon, where the landlady had taken her for a young bride, the thought of nuptial bliss had burned within her, and the further the realisation of this bliss receded, the more uncontrollable her desire became.

Sali, too, felt this desperate longing, for although he had no wish to follow the Fiddler's invitation, it had set his mind in a whirl. In a choking voice he said:

'Let's go inside and have something to eat and drink.'

They entered the parlour, where the only people left were the party of vagabonds, who were seated round a table, eating their humble repast.

'Here come the bride and groom!' cried the Fiddler. 'Rejoice, young people, and plight your troth to each other!'

They allowed themselves to be led to the table, happy of a chance to be able to escape from themselves for a moment. Sali ordered wine and more food to be brought, and a merry party commenced. The sulky young horn-player had made his peace with his unfaithful partner and was fondling her passionately; the other pair of lovers, too, sang and drank and caressed each other lovingly, while the Fiddler and the hunchback played away to their hearts' content.

Sali and Vrenchen sat there without speaking, clasped in each other's arms. Then suddenly the Fiddler called for order and performed a mock ceremony which was meant to represent a wedding. He made them take each other's hands, then bade the assembled company rise and come up one by one to congratulate the young couple and welcome them to the fraternity. They submitted in silence, taking it as a jest, but at the same time trembling in apprehension.

Roused by the strong wine, the little gathering became more and more excited and made more and more noise, until at last the Fiddler gave the order to depart.

'We have a long journey before us,' he cried, 'and it is already past midnight. Come! Let us escort the

bride and bridegroom on their road! I will lead the
way myself and set the pace!'

Their minds in a whirl, the poor young lovers did
not know which way to turn, and helplessly allowed
themselves to be put at the head of the procession.
Behind them came the other two couples, and the
hunchback brought up the rear, his instrument over
his shoulder.

The Fiddler started off down the hillside, playing
his violin like one possessed, and the others skipped
along behind him, laughing and singing. On they went
through the night, past silent fields and meadows and
into Sali's and Vrenchen's own village, where all had
long been sleeping.

As they made their way through the quiet streets
and past their homes, they were gripped by a feeling of
wild abandon and danced along madly behind the Fiddler, kissing each other, laughing and weeping. They
danced their way up the ridge where the three fields
had lain, and when they reached the top, the Fiddler
played in an even greater frenzy, leaping about like a
demon and daring his companions to vie with him in
his revelry. Even the hunchback joined in, groaning
under the weight of his burden, and the whole hillside
echoed as though with the noise of the Witches'
Sabbath.

Holding Vrenchen tightly in his arms, Sali, who was
the first to regain his senses, forced her to stand still;
then, to stop her wild singing, he kissed her firmly on
the lips. They stood there in silence, listening as the
wedding revellers wended their noisy way across the
field and disappeared into the distance along the river
bank, without even noticing that the young lovers

were no longer with them. The sound of the Fiddler's
violin, the girls' laughter and the boys' shouts still rang
out for a time into the night, until they too, died away
and all was still.

'We have escaped from the others,' said Sali, 'but
how can we escape from ourselves? How can we ever
live apart?'

Vrenchen could find no answer. She clung to him,
her breast heaving.

'Should we not go back to the village?' he said. 'Perhaps someone there would take care of you. Then tomorrow you could be on your way again.'

'Without you?'

'You must forget me.'

'That I shall never do! Could you forget me?'

'That is not the point, my sweetheart,' said Sali,
stroking her flushed cheeks as she leant against him and
tossed her head feverishly from side to side. 'It is you I
am thinking of. You are young, and things are bound
to work out for you, wherever you are.'

'And what about you, you old man?'

'Come!' said Sali impulsively, leading her away. After
a few yards they stopped again and embraced each
other. The silence of the world was music in their souls;
the only sound came from the river flowing softly by.

'How beautiful it is everywhere! Can you hear something that sounds like singing and bells chiming?'

'It's the water rushing past. There's no other sound.'

'But there is, listen! It's all around us!'

'It must be our own blood in our ears.'

They listened for a while to the mysterious sounds,
whether imagined or real, which issued from the great
stillness around them, or which they confused with the

magic effects of the moonlight that seemed to hover above the white autumn mist which covered the ground.

Suddenly Vrenchen remembered something, and searching in the bodice of her dress, she exclaimed:

'I bought a souvenir that I wanted to give you.'

And taking the simple ring, she placed it on his finger.

Sali took out his own ring, put it on Vrenchen's hand and said:

'We both had the same thought.'

Holding up her hand in the pale moonlight, Vrenchen examined her ring.

'Oh, how lovely it is!' she cried, smiling. 'Now we are really betrothed—you are my husband and I am your wife! Just let's pretend it's really true for a minute—just until that wisp of cloud has passed across the moon, or until we have counted up to twelve. Kiss me twelve times!'

Sali's love was no less strong than Vrenchen's, but he had never felt that marriage held the inescapable decision between life and death. She, however, saw with passionate intensity either the one or the other possibility, each absolute and unconditional.

But now a new realisation dawned on her, and the emotions of a young girl suddenly turned to the fierce desires of a woman. Sali's embraces became more and more urgent as he held her in his savage grip, covering her with kisses. Vrenchen felt this change in him, and a shudder went through her body, but before the cloud had passed across the face of the moon, she was seized by the same passion. As they caressed each other, their hands came together, and their two rings were joined in an involuntary and symbolic expression of their union.

His heart throbbing, Sali whispered breathlessly:

'There is only one way out for us, Vrenchen. This must be our wedding hour—then we must leave the world behind. Over there is the river—where no one can part us. We shall have given each other our love, whether for a single night or for a lifetime.'

And Vrenchen answered:

'Sali, the same thought has been in my mind hundreds of times—that we should die together and put an end to everything. Promise me that we shall do so!'

'It is all that is left to us,' said Sali, 'for nothing but Death can take you from me now!'

Tears of joy came to her eyes. Then jumping up, she ran as lithe as a deer across the field and towards the river. Sali ran after her, for he thought she was trying to escape from him, while Vrenchen, for her part, thought that he wanted to hold her back. On they ran, one behind the other, and Vrenchen laughed like a runaway child. When they reached the river, they stopped and faced each other.

'Are you sad?'

'No, I'm happy!'

Mindless of their sorrows, they descended the bank and ran along by the water's edge, overtaking the current in their eagerness to find a place to lie. Their one feeling now was of the ecstasy that bound them; the final parting that was to follow seemed but a triviality, and they thought as little about it as a wastrel thinks about the morrow when he has spent his last penny.

'My flowers shall show me the way!' cried Vrenchen. 'Look, they are withered already!' And plucking the posy from her breast, she threw it into the water and sang:

'But sweeter than the almond is the love I bear to thee!'

'Stop!' cried Sali suddenly. 'Here is your bridal bed!'

They had come to a path that led from the village down to the river. Here there was a landing-stage to which a large boat, piled high with hay, was tied up. Feverishly Sali began to untie the mooring ropes. Taking hold of his arm, Vrenchen said with a smile:

'What are you doing? Do you mean to steal the farmers' hay-barge?'

'This is their wedding-gift to us—a floating bridal chamber and a bed such as no bride has ever seen! Besides, they will find their property down by the weir, which is where they would take it in any case, and they will never know what happened. Look, it's rocking and wants to move out into the stream!'

The boat was lying in fairly deep water a few yards from the bank. Lifting Vrenchen high in the air, Sali carried her through the water towards the boat, but she hugged him so tightly, caressing him and squirming about in his arms like a fish, that he could hardly keep his footing in the strong current. She tried to dip her hands and face in the water, exclaiming:

'Let me touch the cool water too! Do you remember how cold and wet our hands were when we first gave them to each other? We were catching fish then; now we're going to become fish ourselves—two fine fat ones!'

'Be quiet, you little witch,' said Sali, striving to keep his balance as he carried his struggling sweetheart through the water, 'or we'll be swept away!'

He lifted her on to the boat and pulled himself up after her; then he helped her to climb on to the sweet-smelling hay and got up beside her. And as they sat there together, the boat drifted slowly out into the middle of the current and floated gently downstream.

The river wended its way through tall, dark woods which cast their shadow over the water, and through open country; sometimes it glided through peaceful villages, sometimes past lonely cottages. In parts of its course it flowed so slowly that it became like a tranquil lake, and the boat almost stopped; in other parts it surged past craggy rocks and left the sleeping banks quickly behind.

With the glow of dawn a town came into view, its steeples rising above the silver waters. The setting moon cast a shaft of light on to the surface of the water, and the boat drifted down the river along this gold-red path. As it approached the town, two pale figures rose in the chill of the September morning and slipped from the dark hulk into the cold waters below, clasped in each other's arms.

A short while afterwards the boat struck a bridge and lodged there, undamaged. The bodies were found later below the town, and when their identity had been established, the newspapers reported that a young couple belonging to two impoverished and degenerate families which had been locked in a bitter feud, had drowned themselves in the river after dancing happily the whole afternoon and enjoying themselves at a fair.

It was also assumed that there was a connection between this event and an incident in the same area involving a hay-barge which had drifted downstream into

the town with no one on board: it appeared that the
couple had stolen the boat in order to celebrate their
sinful union. And this, the writer added, could only be
seen as just one more proof of the growing depravity
and immorality of the times.